GUERRILLA

Guerrilla

A Novel

by

LORD DUNSANY

THE BOBBS-MERRILL COMPANY
PUBLISHERS

INDIANAPOLIS   91172   NEW YORK

FOREWORD

THE man who told this tale had got to London, after sufferings of which he never spoke. He was full of hope, a hope so firm that it induced in him almost a kind of gaiety, and certainly a fine energy. He was an uncle of the lad of whom the story chiefly tells. And the story went something like this: without details, with few names of persons or places, nor even the name of the country. Something had taught him to mention names rarely, and to believe that German ears were always listening, even in London.

But it is not the names or the places or the lesser details that are important. And I cannot be sure enough that this violent story of mine of this little fraction of the rage of a furious year will last to be read in the calm days that shall come after our war, for me to describe with any more exactitude this story, magnificent in its spirit and hope and courage.

GUERRILLA

I

THE army had surrendered, the Germans were through the mountains; and what was always referred to as The Land, as though in reality there were no other country to care about, was one more particle of the German loot. To men accustomed to horses, the Germans had come with amazing speed; to men who never spoke of a distance by measurement, but only of the time it took to get from one place to another, their pace was bewildering. One day they were ringing their bells in the little capital, for news of a fine stand that one of their divisions had made. The next day the Germans were marching down the main street.

Puzzled citizens were walking slowly about the central square; and, when a man stood up on a dais where tea was usually served in the afternoons, and began to make a speech, there was soon a crowd. A few politenesses and little flatteries, and he began to explain the position. England had begun the war, he explained, by attacking Poland. The Germans had therefore had to establish a defensive position there; and, in order to make this impregnable, they had to occupy several other countries as a purely temporary measure. To these countries they came for the countries' own good, as otherwise England would seize them, and this was particularly the case with The Land. Hitler himself had

9

appointed a Protector for The Land, and, if he were duly obeyed, his protection would be equally shared by all, and The Land would have the advantage of the highest possible culture, which was only to be enjoyed by those nations banded together in the new European order established by Adolf Hitler. Resistance would be most severely punished, and was also useless, because they had no rifles, and could not possibly fight in the plains, where they would be helpless against the big German tanks. Anyone who went into the mountains would be foolish, because the German aeroplanes, of which there were hundreds of thousands, could go over the mountains as easily as tanks could go over the plains, and even quicker. The army had surrendered, and it was the duty of all civilians to maintain order and wear a quiet demeanour. The Germans wished them well, and he reciprocated by calling for three cheers for Adolf Hitler. He got a cheer from a few; the rest were silent; and three men who had not cheered were led away by German policemen and instantly shot.

The sound of the volley from a small wood near by, in which the men were shot, came, as it was intended to come, to the central square. But instead of having an effect, as the Germans had planned, it had two effects. One effect was the one the Germans intended, merely fear; but on most of the crowd the effect was one that the Germans have never understood.

There was no protest: all in the square were unarmed. The crowd moved quickly away from the speaker, and slowly out of the square; Srebnitz was among them, the nephew of the old man who told this story in London. Srebnitz had just left school and not yet gone to the university, where he was due for his first term in a fortnight's time. He went away mournfully, about halfway between the two moods I have mentioned. He went back to his home, where he lived with his father and mother in a street not far from the square. He went into the room in which his parents were sitting. His mother looked up quickly when he came in, but said nothing. His father did not even look up. At last Srebnitz spoke.

"Is The Land finished?" he said.

His father smiled grimly. "That is impossible," he said.

"Oh, no," was his mother's answer to Srebnitz.

"Why is it impossible?" asked the boy.

"After three thousand years of freedom," said his father, "it cannot be lost."

"But why not?" his son asked.

"You don't know what three thousand years are," his father replied. "In all that time freedom grows so hard that it is like a piece of rock at the core of a mountain, that cannot be broken or ground away, and cannot disappear ever."

"We have no rifles," said his son.

His father sighed and shrugged his shoulders, but would not abandon his point. His wife said nothing, but agreed with him and hoped that their son would share his father's point of view. But the son only repeated all the arguments about mountains and tanks and plains that the man had

used who had spoken in the square, although he hated the
man; and his father had nothing to say against these arguments; for tanks and planes were all new to him, or rather
new to his thought: he had heard about them for more
than twenty years, but he had not thought of them much.
Deep in his thoughts was the old thought of The Land and
its three thousand years of story, and he felt that aeroplanes
may come and go, and all other inventions that had been on
trial as yet for so short a time, while The Land must go on
for ever. But he could only repeat that The Land was eternal, and had nothing whatever to say to help Srebnitz when
he asked how they could help her. Srebnitz had an air-gun,
which for the last five years had been the principal treasure
of his life. He used to go up with it into the mountain beyond the city, and sometimes, very rarely, shoot a coney.

"I have my air-gun," he said.

But his father only smiled. Why? thought the boy, and
felt the smile was unjust. His father could tell him of no
actual deed, no material thing, that could be of any practical
use. And when he mentioned one, small but at least something, he only met with derision. Almost he flared up, to
defend himself and his air-gun, but he saw his mother's face
looking so sad, and his country's case seemed to himself so
hopeless, that he walked mournfully away and went up to
his own room.

In an air that was vibrating with events, every sound
seemed to be magnified. He heard the bronze knocker on
their door send echoes through the house, and the trifle

altered his mood as a pebble may alter the face of a pond.
And it altered it for the better, for his hopes were then at
the lowest at which they had ever been, and any change was
good. He ran down the stairs with the speed of a man who
is expecting a visitor, though he expected nothing; and,
opening the door, he found his friend Gregor, a young man
who had been at school with him and had left for the university the term before. He was standing there, with his
handsome southern face, dark hair and keen eyes, and
Srebnitz saw in an instant that that expression of misery,
that was in nearly all faces now, was not in Gregor's face.
Two women passed, both with tears in their eyes, but
Gregor's eyes were flashing, as they usually were when he
talked with Srebnitz, and Srebnitz's spirits rose at the sight:
here seemed some glimmer of hope where there had been
none at all, a light in complete darkness. Perhaps Srebnitz
was volatile, but these were times in which all men were
volatile.

"What are you going to do?" asked Gregor.

Do? There seemed nothing to do. Yet the very question
cheered Srebnitz. Gregor must think that something could
be done. Srebnitz had the admiration for Gregor that boys
have for an elder boy, picked from among other elder boys
as one standing out even among them. All elder boys are
wonderful to the younger ones: indeed half a year's growth
is a phenomenon making a real, and rather mysterious,
difference, such as more rarely exists among full-grown
men; and, added to these few months of extra age, was the

superiority of Gregor himself, which made him stand out even among his own exact contemporaries; or at least so it seemed to Srebnitz. The world knows nothing of the great figures between eighteen and nineteen years old, as viewed by those between seventeen and eighteen. Sometimes such a lad fulfils his promise, and dazzles the world as he dazzled the boys that knew him: more often the chances of life and his character, interwoven together, produce something that soon fades in the light of the years, while a boy that nobody quite remembers has at length from mankind the kind of honour that ought to have gone to the captain of the football eleven. But it was not in football that Gregor shone, a game with which they toyed rather than played, nor even at their own national game; it was not in athletics at all that Gregor excelled in such a way as to win the admiration of Srebnitz, but in an intense brightness of mind, which could go to the heart of poetry as the humming-bird hawk-moth goes to the hearts of the flowers, which great numbers of them were doing every evening at the time that the Germans arrived.

It was from Gregor's conversation that Srebnitz found whole new worlds. He was all to Srebnitz that Chapman had been to Keats. He quoted to him not only from Byron, of whom Srebnitz knew already, but told him that there were other poets in the world beyond The Land. He had astounded Srebnitz with Coleridge. He had told him, roughly, in their own language, the story of Kubla Khan. Gregor himself did not know much English, and his story was wholly in prose, but his keen enthusiasm passed the enchantment on. Queer fragments of it stayed in Srebnitz's mind, and grew there like flowers from seeds brought from a far country.

"There were very old voices there," said Gregor, "that prophesied war." That was one of the sounds of a strange dark scene that remained in Srebnitz's imagination for ever.

Another fragment told of a girl singing. "She sang of Mount Abora," said Gregor, with eyes shining. Had Srebnitz had any idea of where Mount Abora was, the effect on his imagination, and indeed on the memories of his life, would have been weaker; as it was, the gardens and forests of a new and very wonderful land were added to the store that his mind had garnered, and there they lay among all those facts and illusions upon which he looked whenever his eyes turned inwards. And in those gardens was always a girl singing; and far far beyond the gardens and over the forest, a grey shape faint in pale sky, arose the peak of Mount Abora. Had it been shown on the map, it was only a mountain. Had he seen it with his own eyes, it was still but a mountain, a material thing, unenchanted. But a Coleridge told of it, and as translation withered it, and as Gregor brought it to life again, it was a thing so wonderful as to be the theme of a song; and the Abyssinian girl brought it nearer, calling it over the world with a power denied to Mahomet.

And here was Gregor asking what Srebnitz was going to do, as though a free choice were still possible, as though freedom, after all, had not left The Land. What could be done?

"What are you going to do?" asked Srebnitz.

"I am going into the Mountain," said Gregor.

A tramp of marching feet was heard, as the boys went inside. On the way up to Srebnitz's room Gregor explained that an army was gathering there, led by Hlaka, a veteran of an old war, who had gone to the Mountain, and was already among the peaks when the Germans arrived in the capital, and his followers would join him there one by one. Srebnitz listened at first with flaming hopes, but upon them suddenly fell like thunder-showers the arguments of the traitor in the Square: they had no guns, no rifles. All the light suddenly went out of Srebnitz's eyes as they walked across his room to the window. "We have no rifles," said Srebnitz.

"There are plenty there," said Gregor, pointing out over the town.

The marching feet were nearer: it was a battalion of German infantry coming down the street. Gregor opened the window and waved his handkerchief to them and, as they came underneath, shouted *"Sieg heil."*

"What does that mean?" asked Srebnitz, puzzled and mournful.

"I don't know," said Gregor, "but it is something the Germans shout."

"Why do you do it?" asked Srebnitz.

"Because I want one of their rifles," Gregor replied.

Srebnitz looked in astonishment at his face, and saw nothing there but a grim determination. Srebnitz's astonishment had no effect on that look, and it remained there steadfast. Then Srebnitz knew that Gregor had really a plan, and that something could be done. Gregor turned from him again to the window and went on waving his handkerchief, and again shouted "*Sieg heil.*" It was long before Gregor turned from the window.

"Every man who brings a rifle," he said, "will be admitted to Hlaka's army."

"One of theirs?" asked Srebnitz.

"One of theirs," said Gregor.

Gregor went to the window again and leaned out and looked down the street after the German battalion. He was no longer waving his handkerchief, and he had a different look in his eyes now. Then he closed the window and turned back to Srebnitz.

"And bring some cartridges if you can," he said. "Rifles are no good without cartridges."

"You are really going?" said Srebnitz.

"I am going tonight," said Gregor.

"How lovely," cried Srebnitz.

"Not at all," Gregor answered. "It is very terrible indeed. When I go there will be reprisals, and they will kill people."

"They will kill innocent people?" gasped Srebnitz.

"I don't know what 'innocent people' means," said Gregor. "They will kill people who have done nothing, because I have done my duty. It is most terrible. It will be as though I had plunged my knife into their hearts. But Our People must be free. Or dead. Many have died in three thousand years. But all who lived have been free. We must be free."

Srebnitz gazed at him and hope came among his dreams, as Gregor had once brought Mount Abora into his imagination.

Gregor went on. "Say *Heil Hitler* wherever you go. The little monkey likes it, and his slaves insist on it. Say it whenever you speak to anyone, and whenever you stop speaking to them. I waved from your window and shouted one of their shouts, so that they shan't come here first, when they come to shoot people. But they'll come here some day, and it's better to die on the Mountain. They'll kill your father and mother when they come."

Srebnitz gasped. "They wouldn't do that!" he exclained.

Gregor turned round on Srebnitz, full in front of him, close.

"You must understand the Germans," he said. "Get your mind clear. If they are harmless decent people, you don't want to kill them, at least not the way we shall do it. You must find out what they are, before you know how to treat them. You don't shoot your neighbours' dogs; you do shoot the fox. Find out what they are, for yourself; then you'll know how to treat them. When you are ready, come to the Mountain."

The Mountain was quite close to the town: they could see its peaks clear from the window, and could sometimes see moving dots that were wild sheep: nothing else lived there.

"I am ready now," said Srebnitz.

"No," said Gregor. "You believe what I say. That's nice of you. But wait till you know it for yourself. You will fight better that way. You will fight then as we shall have to fight. This isn't war, you know. No battles and medals and strategy. This is guerrilla. This is killing, as we kill animals. That is to say, as butchers in the town, and as hunters up in the Mountain."

To his astonishment Srebnitz saw that Gregor was going. He gazed at him. Gregor had told him nothing of what he was to do, and he had looked to Gregor for the minutest instructions. Hoping yet to be told how to act, he said:

"But how do I get a rifle?"

"You have a knife?" asked Gregor.

"Yes," answered Srebnitz.

And, as Srebnitz said that, Gregor's face lit up with a most charming smile, which lingered upon it as he walked across the room and was shining there still as he went out of the door, looking back into Srebnitz's face.

II

SREBNITZ went downstairs to the room where his parents sat, full of his new hopes. "There's an army up in the Mountain," he said. "It will free The Land."

Half an hour earlier his father was telling him there was hope, when he had none. Now he was instructing his father in the same thing, as though it were new. Naturally they did not quite agree: the old man was not going to sit at a desk and be instructed by his son, especially in a matter in which he had so recently been the instructor.

"Who told you that?" his father asked. And when the boy said that it was the brilliant Gregor, he only found that Gregor meant nothing to his father, and that he did not believe in the army. Then he mentioned the name of Hlaka, and that did impress his father. But where was Hlaka? How could he get to him? Suddenly there surged back into Srebnitz's mind the horrible words of Gregor, that they would shoot his father and mother. Srebnitz did not believe it; and that was what Gregor had meant when he had said that he was not yet ready to go to the Mountain. He did not believe it, and yet the thought came back with a deadening shock. For it was a dreadful thing to think of, even though it could not be true. As they talked there came knocks on the door, strangely different from Gregor's knocks. They sounded so angrily impatient that Srebnitz ran to open the door. There was a Prussian major there.

"*Heil Hitler,*" said Srebnitz.

"*Heil Hitler,*" replied the major.

It was true then; they did talk like that.

"*Sprechen Sie Deutsch?*" said the major.

"*Nein,*" said Srebnitz, for the words they had spoken so far were the only German words that Srebnitz knew. And then the Prussian officer spoke to him with a fairly good accent in his own Near Eastern language.

"I am billeted here," said the officer.

"Won't you come in?" said Srebnitz, for he was of a polite though fierce people, and he brought the officer into the sitting-room. Srebnitz's mother got up from her chair timidly, but the old man refused to move. This man was not his guest, and he came of a free people.

"I am billeted here," said the Prussian officer.

The old man nodded his head; he was powerless to keep the German out.

"We have come to safeguard our own frontiers from aggression," said the officer, "and for the good of your own Land."

The old man turned slightly in his chair, away from the German.

"It is so everywhere," said the German to Srebnitz. "The old have not yet learned, but all the young are for Hitler."

Srebnitz was silent for a few moments, and then he said: "*Heil Hitler.*"

"*Heil Hitler,*" repeated the German.

One eyebrow of Srebnitz's father rose slightly; his mother sat silent.

"Show the officer to your bedroom," said his father. "You must sleep here on the floor."

Srebnitz did as his father told him. The German seemed pleased with the room, or with Srebnitz's politeness to him, and almost smiled. He was silent a few moments, evidently thinking what he could do for Srebnitz. Then he said:

"Tell your father and mother to change their minds while there is still time. Now I will go and send round my kit."

And he went amiably down the stairs.

An officer, thought Srebnitz, an officer. He would not have a rifle. And he decided to bide his time.

When Srebnitz went downstairs again his father said to him: "Why did you say that?"

He spoke in a strange grim voice that was new to Srebnitz. Like a judge speaking. As though on behalf of many alive and dead he questioned his son.

And the son replied with the words that Gregor had said to him: "This is not a war, Father. It is guerrilla."

And his father seemed to have understood at once, and said no more, but sat looking into the fire and often smiling quietly. Then Srebnitz remembered that he kept his knife in his room, and went up to get it before the German returned. It was a thin knife, about eight inches long, in a sheath of red leather. It is the usual custom of the people of that land to keep their knives about as sharp as we keep our razors, and Srebnitz's knife was like the rest, but he drew it out and honed it with a little stone, to make sure, and stropped it on leather, until the German came back and knocked with his angry knocks again on the door. Then Srebnitz sheathed his knife and hid it under his clothes; and always after that wore it hung on a strip of leather next to his skin. He ran downstairs and looked in at the sitting-room, on his way to open the door. Perhaps his mother guessed why he went upstairs, or perhaps she merely wondered.

"Did you go upstairs to make the room comfortable for the officer?" she asked.

"Yes," said Srebnitz, "or for one of them. I went to get this."

And he opened his shirt and showed the top of the handle of the knife, a carved piece of wild-sheep's horn inlaid with little pieces of silver wire. His mother nodded, but never said a word. His father saw too, and said nothing. The knocks on the door came again, more angry and longer, and Srebnitz hurried to open the door.

"*Heil Hitler*," said Srebnitz.

"*Heil Hitler*," replied the officer.

Yes, they had only been parted for little over five minutes, and it was evidently quite correct to say this all over again.

The German had an orderly with him, with both hands full of kit. No rifle amongst it, Srebnitz noticed. This meant that he must get his rifle elsewhere, and he was glad for his parents' sake.

Then he remembered that he had not passed on this man's warning to his parents. He showed the way to the staircase and, leaving the officer to go up with the orderly and the kit, went into the sitting-room. Somehow he could not think of words in which to tell what he had to say, so he repeated the German officer's own words, warning his parents to change their minds while there was still time. But the old man only smiled and slightly shook his head. He would have done the same if invited to play football. He was too old for such changes. His wife smiled a little too, and sighed once, and then they heard the feet of the major returning down the stairs.

One often hears of a typical Englishman, a typical soldier, a typical bus-conductor, but very rarely sees any of these types, and when seen they seem slightly absurd; a typical man is in fact a caricature. But this officer was a typical Prussian officer: his face was large and red, and there were hundreds of red veins in it; his body was very plump, although not fat, except for his neck; and the line of his neck went straight to the top of his head, with no bulge any-where, except for the fat of the neck. His neck was red like his face, and his moustache was much cared for: one could not say it was well cared for; it was rather as though a man had employed several gardeners to plant nettles and weeds, or wild jungle-growths, in orderly rows in a garden. His moustache was a dark shade of yellow, and his eyes were blue, and there were bright red veins in his eyes, as well as in his face. At first sight of him you thought of a savage from cannibal lands, who had been drinking blood all his life; but that was a first impression that could linger only a moment, for a second glance showed that, far from being a savage, he had been drilled night and day ever since he was eight, and was as far removed from the natural savage as a performing ape that has been all its life in a circus is removed from his happy brothers still at large in the woods. Though he gave orders all day now, he made every movement as though the trainer were still behind him, and the trainer's whip over his head.

Supper was now preparing and, as the German saw his hostess's preparations, a brighter scarlet seemed to shine in the veins of his eyes. No shortage of food had come as yet to The Land. Srebnitz was out of the room when the others sat down to supper. He had gone to get an armful of clothes from his bedroom, to throw them down in the corner in which he was going to sleep. He had scarcely been gone three minutes when he returned with his bundle; and the quarrel had already occurred. The old lady had said grace before sitting down to supper, and the German had tolerated that, but had added the name of Hitler. It was not this that had been the cause of the quarrel; this had only caused exasperation: the actual quarrel arose over the precedence that was due to God's name or to Hitler's. They were sitting very silent when Srebnitz returned; and he saw at once that there had been a quarrel, and feared for his parents' lives. It was only a fear awakened by Gregor's words, for he did not yet know the Germans.

The supper was eaten in silence. Beer was brought in silence to the German officer by Srebnitz's father. And then the German relaxed. He relaxed like a traction-engine that has come over the crest of a hill; his movements were smoother, less awkward. At last he smiled, as heavy engines might smile, if their ghosts spoke together at night, when man had gone. "After all," he said ingratiatingly to Srebnitz's mother, "what do we know of these great figures? It is but for us to obey."

Still he got no response.

"A curious people," he said aloud, but in German, so as not to give them offence.

Srebnitz watched every minute go by, and hoped the end of the evening might come, before either his father or mother had said something that the German would never forgive, if they had not done so already. As soon as the first dimness strayed into the room he went and lay down on his heap of clothes in the corner, though the German was still at the table. Somehow the mere movement had more than the effect that he hoped, and the little party broke up, the German going upstairs and Srebnitz's father and mother going soon to their own bedroom.

All the sounds in the streets outside were changed: there were more feet, fewer voices. Sometimes Srebnitz heard a shout far off. The whole volume of sound was different; the very voice of the city was altered. As none of the voices to which he listened told anything in words, and as none of the dim echoes of sounds that reached him told anything to his reason, Srebnitz listened all the more acutely, bringing his imagination to the aid of his ears, and he lay long awake in the sorrowful city. Suddenly in the night the city's voice changed again, and changed so sharply that Srebnitz awoke. What did it say this time? Still he could not tell. But its voice was alert and horrified.

The Prussian went out next morning without his breakfast.

"Mother," said Srebnitz as they sat over their own breakfast, "you nearly quarrelled with him last night. Please don't. He forgave you. But, if he had not, Gregor says . . ."

"He insulted God," said his mother.

"What did he say?" asked Srebnitz, thinking that perhaps he might explain it away.

"He said He was not a European," she answered.

"But is He?" asked Srebnitz.

"It was not that," his mother replied. "But he implied very clearly that he himself was a European and, better than that, a Prussian."

"But he is," said Srebnitz.

"And therefore superior to God," his mother continued.

"He was joking," said the boy.

"We don't joke like that," said his mother.

"No," said Srebnitz. "But don't be hard on him if he can't see things as we do. Because Gregor says . . ."

"What does Gregor say?" said his mother, though not in a voice that sounded as though she sought instruction from Gregor.

"Gregor says . . ." But somehow what Gregor had said seemed rather absurd, and he could not bring himself to repeat it. "Well, he'll be hungry when he comes back," he said. "Let's give him a good breakfast. We must make him comfortable while he is here. Perhaps they will go soon."

"Perhaps," said his mother.

The German soon returned. Srebnitz had been thinking that his impression that his face was red could not be really true. It was a bright, bright red. He strode into the room and made a speech. He said, speaking so as to have been heard by a large audience, had one been there, that the people of The Land were a savage people. "We come to the country for its own good," he said, "and in order to protect it from England. And how have they shown their gratitude? What have they done?" He paused, then shouted louder, "What have they done?"

Then Srebnitz saw that an answer was needed, and said, "We don't know."

"You don't know," repeated the German. "No, because it is incredible. You accursed people have murdered a German sentry."

"It is incredible," said Srebnitz.

It was the *mot juste*. But his mother said nothing. The Prussian looked at her, to hear what she would say. Still she said nothing.

"Very well," he said suddenly, and strode out of the house.

"That's right," said Srebnitz when he had gone. "I was afraid you might say something to make him angry. We must be rather quiet while he is in this mood. In a day or two it will blow over."

And then his father came in to have his breakfast: he had been upstairs making the German's bed. He had heard the shouting and knew what had happened. He said nothing as he came in, but his face seemed to wear resignation, like an ancient national dress.

"Gregor has killed a sentry," said Srebnitz.

And the old man nodded his head. He sat down to his breakfast and seemed to be waiting for something. Presently the major returned with three armed soldiers. He marched in, and they behind him. The Prussian had a paper in his hand and at once began to shout. The gist of his shouting was that Aryan life was sacred; that the German people, the most cultured in the world, knew this, but there were inferior races that did not know it. To these races the Germans must act like parents and teach the simple lesson; stern parents, until the lesson was learned. When these good lessons were learned, all the world would be happy; meanwhile there must be reprisals. Fifty persons must be shot to atone for the murder of the sentry. The behaviour of his host had been correct: it was therefore a pleasure to spare him. Young Srebnitz, like the youth of the whole world, would learn to love Hitler if he did not already. The behaviour of his mother was incorrect.

He turned round on his heel and marched out of the house, and the soldiers led away the old woman. Her husband followed them. Srebnitz too followed as far as the door. For one moment all three soldiers had their backs to him. He looked as earnestly at their large shoulder-blades as he had ever looked at anything. Then one of them made a half-turn, and Srebnitz seemed to have changed his mind.

He did not realise then that he would never see either of his parents again. He did not yet wholly believe Gregor.

His mother was shot dead that afternoon. His father had insisted on accompanying her to the wall before which she had to stand; so the Germans had laughed, and shot him too.

That evening when Srebnitz heard what had happened, the despair of the day before had wholly left him; there was scarcely even grief in his heart, and no fear and no other emotion except one, which wholly filled it, a deep and ardent yearning to get a rifle.

III

THERE is a story of Kipling's about a man whose pet ape tore his master's wife to pieces from jealousy, and, knowing he had been naughty, kept away from the man for some days, till the man lured him back with little kindnesses, and finally killed him.

The position between Srebnitz and the Prussian major on the day after the reprisals was, in their attitude towards each other, somewhat that of the man and the ape, after the ape had killed the woman. Did Srebnitz feel resentment? the major wondered. He did not seem to; and yet the officer, from his knowledge of psychology, which he had once studied at a German university, suspected that

Srebnitz might have such a feeling, even although it was reasonably groundless. Men do not act always from reason alone, he had once been taught. And yet he reasoned with Srebnitz.

In war, he explained to him, certain things were necessary, and logically followed on other things. And he explained to Srebnitz the usage of reprisals, with the exactitude of a chess player explaining an opening. Srebnitz agreed at once. The position was clear enough to the major, but he was a little surprised to find that it was so clear to a man who had not the advantage of German culture. And so he explained it all over again, which logically was what he ought to have done if Srebnitz had not understood him, but not when he did understand. Well, there was no harm in making sure; and the clear logic of his argument had a soothing effect on the major's own mind, which was slightly teased now and again with doubts as to whether Srebnitz was as well disposed to him as he appeared, and as he certainly ought to be. If one loses one's queen at chess to an important piece on the other side, one does not bear resentment to that piece.

Srebnitz did not appear to act in any such foolish way, and logically ought not to do so; so why suppose that he did? And yet the fact remained that nobody could tell what anyone outside Germany would think about anything. And this fact, however absurd, should be borne in mind, for a reasonable man must never neglect a fact. In Germany the moment the Fuehrer spoke on the

wireless on any subject, one knew what everyone thought on
that subject: in an ordered country it must be so; then all
men acted the same way, because they thought the same
way, and their action came with the weight of a single blow,
eighty million people striking together; and such a blow
must be victorious. It was very simple; it was the difference
between organization and running wild, the difference between culture and savagery, and incidentally the difference
between victory and occupation. The occupied countries
must be taught this now, like children in school; those as
yet unoccupied must learn by defeat. "So," said the Prussian out loud. Srebnitz smiled. Was it a natural smile?
All that the major and his forbears had learned for three
generations said that it was, for how else should other peo-
ples act towards Prussians? But some older, simpler lore,
that had not studied psychology, seemed to be doubting that
smile. One more word to Srebnitz.

But Srebnitz said, "I must cook your dinner now. It will
not be cooked quite as well as it used to be."

"Naturally," said the Prussian.

Then Srebnitz went to the kitchen to do his best.

A foolish remark about the cooking. How could a man
cook as well as a woman? Only an uncultured people,
thought the major, would trouble to point out such a thing.
Did the boy think he would punish him for the inferior cooking? Germans were not unreasonable.

Srebnitz brought in the dinner, and the meat was tough,
as the officer had expected. He made no complaint. He

knew well enough that a woman's place was the kitchen. Even a German man would not try to compete there, still less an uncultured man. The woman had cooked well. But such things could not be considered in war. Reprisals came first. Indeed it was by reprisals that Germany must keep her hold on the occupation of the world. Decent cooking would follow.

The major and Srebnitz ate together. Often Srebnitz's hand would move to his waist and linger there for a moment.

"Your stomach aches?" asked the Prussian.

"No, no, no," said Srebnitz. "Yes, it does." And suddenly Srebnitz realised that he must have been fondling the handle of the knife that was under his shirt.

It might have been an awkward twenty minutes while the Prussian major and Srebnitz ate their dinner, were it not for the young man's frequent smiles. One thing prevented the military shrewdness of the major from detecting any falsity in those smiles, and that was that they were entirely sincere: whenever Srebnitz smiled he was thinking of his rifle that he was going to get and take away to the Mountain. The Mountain and its bright freedom, and the free men whom he would meet there, filled his mind as flowers are filled with sunlight. After dinner the major marched out. And Srebnitz was left in the lonely house, to sit by the kitchen fire and make his plans. And the more he planned, the harder it seemed to be, till the daring act that should win the rifle seemed the easiest step of all. First of all, the Germans had imposed a curfew within half an hour of sunset, as one of the punishments for the death of their sentry. This would mean his arrest if found at night in the streets at all, even without carrying a German rifle, and there would be a bayonet with it too. There would be a long way to go through the streets from the place where the sentry would be. And then there was a moon about four days old: that would not help things either. Srebnitz's plans had not progressed very far when there came a knock at the door. It was not the terrible Gestapo; in fact it was evidently not a German at all. Srebnitz could not guess who it could be; and, had he guessed for long, the man he saw in the doorway would have been the last of his guesses. It was Gregor.

"Gregor!" Srebnitz exclaimed.

Gregor smiled.

"They have killed my father and mother," said Srebnitz.

"Yes, and mine," said Gregor. "Our fathers and mothers were lost when the Germans first came. We are probably all lost. But The Land will be free."

"I will get the rifle," said Srebnitz.

"That is right," said Gregor. "It will be beautiful up on the Mountain with a rifle. Their sentries wear bandoliers. Remember to bring the bandolier."

"There's a curfew."

"I came to tell you about that," said Gregor. "You must go by moonlight, so that the sentry can see you. You couldn't get close in the dark. Have a piece of white paper in your hand. Say *'Erlaubnis'*—that means 'permit'—and give it to him."

"But when he reads it?" said Srebnitz.

"He must never read it," said Gregor.

"No," said Srebnitz. "And then?"

"Then take his rifle and bandolier, and take off your boots, and hide till the moon goes down. There will be nobody near at the time, because you will choose a time when the sentry is alone, before you take your permit to him. Tie your boots round your neck; you will want them on the Mountain."

"Where will I hide?" asked Srebnitz.

"The two best places are the wood and the public gardens," said Gregor, for a pinewood came right into the town. "So avoid those two. The Germans will search them as soon as they miss their sentry; there are plenty of little gardens among the houses; you know them all; and you can move on from one to another whenever the street is quiet."

Srebnitz did not speak, but gazed thoughtfully into the fire, for they had come to the kitchen.

"Well?" said Gregor.

"I was thinking of the rifle and bayonet," said Srebnitz.

"Don't bring the bayonet," said Gregor. "Hlaka doesn't want them. The Germans will be twenty, and even fifty, to one, when we fight, so we can't sail in with the bayonet."

"Fifty to one?" said Srebnitz.

"Perhaps a hundred to one," said Gregor. "But that doesn't trouble Hlaka. He makes up the difference by brains. But you must use your brains, or Hlaka will flog you."

Perhaps a troubled look came into Srebnitz's face, for he knew he was not as clever as Gregor, and he feared that he might fail the redoubtable Hlaka.

"You've shot coneys, haven't you?" said Gregor.

"A few," said Srebnitz. "But only with an air-gun."

"That's all the brains you need," said Gregor, "and more than enough. A stupid man might kill a coney with a rifle, if he took a long shot, but not with an air-gun. And we don't take long shots."

"From how far do you fire?" asked Srebnitz.

"What is the furthest that you have ever shot a coney?" asked Gregor.

"I shot one once at seventy-five metres," said Srebnitz. "I paced it."

"Then never fire at over seventy metres," said Gregor, "at a German. The first five cartridges, think of your mother; the next five think of your father; and don't waste one. We don't fight battles. If an officer gave an order to open fire at four hundred yards, Hlaka would execute him. No battles; only killing."

"And the rifle," said Srebnitz to remind Gregor of a point from which they had wandered away.

"You must do as you think best," said Gregor. "Indeed you must do that at all times. What I did myself was to carry it through the streets while they were quiet; but I had a small saw with me so that I could saw off the stock in any place where I hid, and carry the barrel under my waistcoat and down my trouser-leg. As it turned out I did not use the saw.

If you do carry it that way it's best to have a stick, and walk
a bit lame. Here is the saw."

And he gave Srebnitz a small sharp saw, only a few
inches long. "Don't bring the stock," he said, "if you
cut it off. You can carve another stock out of a cork-tree.
And now get your air-gun, and let's see how you can
shoot."

While Srebnitz went to get his air-gun Gregor picked
up a large empty match-box and, opening it to make it a
little larger, and walking out of the house and across the
street, set it up on the pavement against the opposite house.
Rifle practice, even of so humble a sort, in the streets of a
conquered city, and among two of the conquered, surprised
Srebnitz as soon as he saw what Gregor had planned. But
Gregor said: "This is how we must live from now on; doing
whatever we like, but choosing our time for it. I will watch
from this window. The moment you hear me shut it, put
your air-gun away."

So Gregor leaned his head out of the window, looking
up and down the street, while Srebnitz fired four shots at
the match-box from six yards inside the house, and every
shot hit it. Then Gregor went and picked the match-box
up, and nothing had disturbed them. As Gregor walked
across the street with the incriminating match-box in his
hand, the idea came to Srebnitz that more might be done
than he had hoped, for the trifle caught his eye, whereas he
had not seen Gregor's journey all the way to the town from
the Mountain.

"What part of the Mountain shall I come to?" asked Srebnitz.

"Any part," said Gregor. "We shall find you. You will be watched all the way. If you carry the rifle in your hand, carry it with the stock foremost."

Then he picked up the air-gun and looked at it.

"That's a nice air-gun," he said. "You could learn to hit a coin at seventy metres with that. Would you like it up on the Mountain?"

"Oh yes," said Srebnitz. "Shall I bring it?"

"No. You will have your rifle to bring," said Gregor. "I'll take it for you. It will go nicely."

And there and then he began to slip it down his waistcoat with the stock uppermost. And Srebnitz gave him several hundred lead slugs in a round tin. These Gregor poured loose into his pockets, and handed back the tin. Then he walked out into the street.

"See you soon," he shouted, and was gone.

Srebnitz went back to his seat by the fire, and back to his thoughts. He had no need of the fire's warmth, for spring was far on its way over all those lands, though the swallows had not yet got as far as England, and the fire was only there for cooking: he sat by the fire so as to see the past in it, which his fancy could sometimes discern in its luminous scenery. He would have liked to have left some flowers upon his parents' graves; but, thinking it all out, he decided that he must choose between that and vengeance.

Then, having made his choice, he went out for a walk

through the streets of the little capital to see where the sentries were: and he went in the direction of the Mountain.
Having found what he wanted, he returned to the house,
stopping on the way at a street corner at which they always
sold flowers, and where men were selling them even yet, and
buying a bunch at the cost of a whole pound of tea, because
he realised that money would not be of much more use to him
for a long time to come. These he brought back to the house
and he began to prepare supper. The major had not yet
returned.

He had not been at work in the kitchen long when a furious knocking was heard at the door and the major was there,
having come back for his supper.

"Heil Hitler," said Srebnitz.

"Heil Hitler," replied the major with the same solemn
face. Would he never get tired of saying this? thought
Srebnitz.

Srebnitz had all his wits about him now, realising that
now, if ever, he must keep them about him. For he meant
to go that night a bit before the moon went behind the Mountain. He could not bring himself to say much to the major,
but he smiled more frequently than he had at dinner. He is
beginning to get over the loss of his parents, thought the
Prussian.

After supper, when he went into the kitchen to put the
plates away, he packed into his pockets and about his clothes
all the tea and sugar there was in the house, and a good deal
of butter and some slices of bacon, and put nearly sixteen

pounds of bread into a sack. Would the major go to bed before the moon set? He could not sit and watch him without letting some trace of his anxiety show through, so he stayed most of the time in the kitchen, where the major heard him moving saucepans and washing plates. Already through a window he saw the moon hanging low. Would beer help? He opened two bottles and placed them beside the major, who was pleased. Then he returned to the kitchen. There he found a sheet of paper and made out his permit; he wrote on it "It is a free Land." For a moment he wondered how to sign it, then signed with his own name.

After what seemed a long time, but may have been only ten minutes, he heard a yawn, then silence, and more silence. His father's old clock sounded loud in it. Suddenly a hope came to him, and he looked quietly into the sitting-room: it was as he hoped and the major had fallen asleep. He scattered some flowers then in rooms and nooks and corners that were especially frequented by memories of his parents, and slipped out into the street, and locked the door on the far side and threw the key away.

The moon was still in the sky, but getting near to the Mountain. The street was quite deserted, and he went quietly in the direction of a little public garden with two gates on the street, over both of which the Germans had put a sentry; and the further of the two sentries was the one that Srebnitz had chosen, because he was the nearer to the Mountain. This meant that he would have to make a detour, up a street to the right and back down another, in order to come to the further sentry without being seen by the nearer. The bit of garden was only a hundred yards long. and the distance between the two sentry-posts was no more than that; but they walked up and down and met in the middle, and would be two hundred yards apart at the end of their beats.

He walked softly, though with his boots on, and felt strangely free. He felt, although the feeling was not crystallised into thought, that Man was opposed to the night, that all his doors and locks and laws were against it. Out-of-doors now, in the silent street, no locks or laws held him. The night was no longer against him; it was his friend: and he was on the side of the night. In the houses freedom was lost now: all who abided by laws in that land abided by German laws: only in the night and on the Mountain were his people still free.

He heard the sound of three men marching, and they seemed more in the night. Then he saw the glint of an electric torch flashing out now and then. To go back would be to lose time, and the moon was getting low. There was a side-street only fifty yards ahead, which he thought he could reach if he hurried, before the men came within hearing of his light feet.

He ran softly and reached it, and ran up the steps of a house on the far side of the side-street and flattened himself against the door; not the first house, but the second, so as to have sufficient start if the patrol turned up that street. They were coming down the far side of the street he had left. If the steps left the pavement to cross the street, he would have ample time to get away from them. But they drew level and kept straight on.

He left the door and continued his journey, and the night seemed more than ever his friend. Then the silence was broken again, this time by a voice, a high voice calling incoherently, somebody singing. The singer was coming towards him out of the distance and dark: it was a drunken man. For a moment Srebnitz was astonished at any sound of festivity in that fallen city; then he realised that it was some poor devil trying to drown the sorrow of Europe in a glass of wine. He came down the street the way the patrol had gone, and Srebnitz heard, as he came nearer, the ruins of songs of his country. He stood still as the man passed him on the other side of the street, so that the man should not hear him and shout to him. And away the wild singing went, sending up fragments of the songs of The Land into the lonely night. For a long while he heard him; then a volley from two or three rifles, and all was quiet.

He heard the sound of more men coming behind him, but that did not trouble him, because he was near the first sentry now and the time was come for him to leave the wide street and turn up to his right, and then soon to his left and to his left again, which would bring him back to the street that he was in, and close to the further sentry. He turned to his right and passed by little gardens, where trees leaned their dark heads out over the railings, trees that seemed friendly to Srebnitz, and free, trees that had never said *Heil Hitler*: freedom was gone from men in The Land, but it seemed still to linger among these leaves.

When he came to his next turning he paused, to hear how far the marching feet had got. If they should turn from the main road where he had turned he would have to make fresh plans, but they went on straight past the turning. Then he turned to his left and was about level with them. As he turned to his left again, he heard them marching on up the wide road, past the far end of the street he had just entered. He was very near the sentry now. He followed the sound of the marching feet for a little way, softly; then he turned back and, as soon as the patrol was out of hearing, walked loudly towards the sentry, whose feet he could now hear, his approach from that direction giving the impression that he must have passed the patrol. He had also timed his walk so as to meet the sentry when he was farthest away from his comrade.

Now he saw the sentry, in such light as there was from the moon, and held out his white paper. Before the sentry challenged Srebnitz called out, *"Erlaubnis,"* and added the word Doctor in his own language, hoping that the Germans would have picked up the word for doctor in any country they entered. If he looked too young for a doctor, the word might be taken to mean that he was in search of one. He waved the paper in the direction in which the patrol had gone, with the implication that they had seen it, and then stretched it out to the sentry, repeating the word *Erlaubnis;* for it was death to be out in the streets after dark without a permit.

Srebnitz came of a race that had held a small country from before the Christian era. They had done this by outstanding courage, and of course by agriculture, but also by cunning. Cunning was honoured among them, probably because they knew, or only dimly felt, that it was one of the pillars upon which their nation rested, and without which their race might have fallen into the dust.

Srebnitz handed the paper to the sentry in the same hand that held the knife: the blade of the knife was under his hand and lying along his wrist. The sentry tried to read it, but there was not enough moonlight. Then Srebnitz spoke of his mother in his own language. Whether the words surged up unbidden out of his thoughts, or whether he spoke to distract the sentry's attention, he did not know himself.

"My mother was always kind," he said.

And then he stabbed the sentry to the heart. The thin knife slipped in easily. The sentry coughed and Srebnitz seized his throat with his left hand for fear that he should cry out: with his right hand he caught the rifle before it could fall, for he knew that the sound of a falling rifle would waken the whole street.

He had forgotten to loosen his boot-strings, so he cut them now with the knife, as the other sentry marched towards the point at which the two of them were accustomed to meet. Srebnitz's sentry seemed quite dead, as he took his hand from his throat. Then he slipped the bandolier over the dead man's head and threw it over his own shoulder, and took off his boots and ran, picking up his small sack of bread as he went, which he had left on the pavement before going up to the sentry. A flash of moonlight on the bayonet as he ran reminded him that Gregor had told him that Hlaka did not need bayonets, and that he was better without it now; so he unfixed it from the rifle and, with a neat knack they have in those parts, threw it into a door, where it stuck; a warning, Srebnitz thought, if the people in the house should be traitors; otherwise a message of hope.

Soon he heard the steps of the patrol again, for he was now overtaking them. So he stopped to think, and to rest; not because he was tired, but in order to have his speed fresh when it might be needed. The other sentry seemed not to have left his beat, and there was no pursuit as yet. It struck Srebnitz then that the safest place for him was as near as possible to the patrol. If they turned he must run: till then they would warn him whenever they passed a sentry, and there would be no more patrols, just behind them.

For a long while he followed the patrol, till it turned down a street that led away from the Mountain. Srebnitz kept straight on, and went now more cautiously.

IV

THE moon was very near to the left side of the Mountain, but it still gave too much light; and Srebnitz looked, as he went, for a place to hide. If the dead sentry was discovered before the moon set, which seemed more than likely, he decided to go on at once, as the certain danger behind would then be greater than the unknown danger in front; but as yet he heard no noise.

He passed a garden, but there seemed no cover there, and the moonlight was all over it. Trees were plentiful along the street, but they were only pepper-trees, with thin trunks. The kind of cover he looked for did not seem to be there, and there were no clouds near the moon. The houses he passed had gardens in front of them, but too minute to grow any trees except almond or orange or peach: none of them gave any cover.

And then he saw a garden so neat and calm and well tended, with the moonlight shining on patches of lemon-blossom, bright in the dark of the leaves, and with something else about it that he could not define, but that charmed him somehow as the echo of chimes that had just stopped ringing on a summer's evening . . . so neat and calm and charming that the idea came to him suddenly that in this house he might find shelter. Without any hesitation or any further thought he went straight up to the door and knocked with his knuckles; nor was there time for any hesitation, for he had been too long in the moonlit street already to hope to go much longer without being seen; and indeed as he knocked he heard marching feet again, between him and the Mountain. He knocked again, a little louder. The door was opened by someone with a knitted shawl over her face, through which she could see.

Srebnitz walked in with his rifle, and his right hand all over blood, and much of the sleeve, and said: "It is for The Land."

The figure behind the shawl nodded, and made a gesture with one hand to an inner door. Then she shut the door on the street, while Srebnitz, still with his rifle in his hand, walked in to the room to which she had pointed. There two old ladies sat knitting, two unmarried sisters. They glanced at Srebnitz's rifle and the blood on his hand, and went on with their knitting.

"It is a fine evening," said one of them.

"Yes," said Srebnitz, and then added what he had said in the doorway: "It is for The Land."

"Yes, yes," said the other old lady. "Are you going to the Mountain?"

"Yes," said Srebnitz. "To Hlaka."

"You must have some tea before you go," she said.

The marching footsteps drew nearer, and another patrol passed the door, as they all listened.

"The moon will set soon," said the old lady who had offered the tea. Her name was Isabella.

"Properly speaking," said her sister, "it will go behind the Mountain. But that will suit quite well."

"I must wash my hands," said Srebnitz very hastily, looking down with a shocked expression at his own right hand in that neat, tidy room.

"That is as you wish," said Isabella. "But, if you are

going to Hlaka, they say—do they not, Angelica?—that he will receive you better with your right hand unwashed."

"That is what I have heard," said Angelica.

"Sophia," called Isabella, "bring us some tea for this young gentleman. And your name?" she said to Srebnitz.

"I think not," said Angelica.

"Very well then, perhaps not," said Isabella.

So Srebnitz remained anonymous.

"My dear young man," said Isabella, "you have no blanket. Nobody goes up to the Mountain without a blanket. It is very cold up there as soon as the sun sets."

"Yes," said Angelica, "he must have a blanket." And she went to get one.

And now Srebnitz heard the sounds of a stir down the road by which he had come, the very sounds that he had been expecting, and he and his hostess knew they had found the sentry.

"You must not go by that road," Isabella said, pointing to the front door. "But Sophia will show you a lane that goes straight to the Mountain."

They were still listening to the noises in the town, when Angelica returned with the blanket, which she made up into a long roll and handed to Srebnitz, and a strip of leather with which to fasten the ends. Srebnitz thanked her and threw it over his right shoulder.

"Not that shoulder," said Angelica. "They never wear it that way."

And Srebnitz realised, rather shamefacedly, that the way he was trying to wear it would get in the way of his rifle. Very soon Sophia came in with the tea, this time with no shawl over her face.

"This is our niece Sophia," said Isabella.

Srebnitz gazed at her and said nothing.

"And your name?" said Sophia when the silence had gone on long enough.

"His name is Monsieur de la Montagne," said Angelica.

"Good evening, Monsieur de la Montague," said Sophia.

"Good evening," said Srebnitz.

Then they all had tea.

"There are lovely flowers up in the Mountain," said Isabella.

"Beautiful, I believe," said Angelica.

Men in thick boots hurried past the house, going up the street that already slanted towards the Mountain, away from the town.

"And are your parents well?" asked Angelica.

"Yes," said Srebnitz.

And the two old ladies sighed.

Even an aeroplane came over after a while, and still there were hurrying Germans in the street.

"Are they going to bomb, do you think?" asked Isabella of her sister.

"Most unlikely," replied Angelica. "They have their own men all over the town."

"So I thought," said Isabella. "I only asked."

"Of course, you never know with Germans," said Angelica.

"No," said Isabella.

And the aeroplane throbbed away towards the Mountain, but the sounds of men in the street did not diminish.

Suddenly there came a roar of knocks on the street-door.

"Quick, Sophia," said Isabella. And she threw two of the four tea-cups into the grate, and their saucers after them, where they lay broken among the ashes. Then she walked to the door of their sitting-room. "To the Mountain," she said to Sophia, "and remember to lock the back-door after you."

Srebnitz wanted to thank her, but there was not time.

"We shall see you again one day," she said. "You can thank us then. Or perhaps there may be reprisals along our street. If so we shall meet again where there are no Germans."

"My dear!" exclaimed Angelica. "Beethoven!"

"Yes, yes. Of course," said Isabella. "I should have excepted him."

The knocking came again, and shook the whole door, and plaster began to fall from where the hinges were straining. Isabella walked slowly down the few yards of passage, and called out, "Who is there?"

"Police," came the shouted answer. "Open at once."

"Certainly," said Isabella.

Sophia and Srebnitz were in the kitchen now, and the door was shut behind them. As Isabella opened the front door, Sophia opened the back. As the Germans entered the house she picked up part of a ham, then followed Srebnitz out of the back door and locked it from the outside. They were in a little garden now, glistening with fruit-trees. Sophia handed the ham to Srebnitz to put into his sack, which now also held his boots, as they walked through the garden. She walked fast, but without anxiety, for it was a long way round to the back of the house by any way except by the back door. They came to a small wicket, which Sophia opened, and they were in a narrow lane leaned over by lemon trees, and orange and peach and wisteria.

For a little while the moon shone faintly on white blossoms; then Srebnitz and Sophia came to the darkness where the moon was hid by the Mountain.

"I have brought another blanket for you," said Sophia. And Srebnitz saw that she had it draped over her. He was glad of that, for he had decided that, with all the blood on his sleeve, it would be no use hiding the rifle as Gregor had done. If found by daylight, he was sure to be shot: if found by night without a permit, it would be the same thing. So it was better to have his rifle handy, and the blanket might do to hide it from aeroplanes. He was troubled about Sophia; indeed he was vaguely troubled from the first moment he saw her; but here she was out in a dark night, in a town full of Germans; nor would it have been any better, but worse, if the dark night had been lit.

He wanted her to go back, but the Germans were there. He was troubled too about the old ladies, whose kindness seemed too fragile to endure in such an age as this: the Germans would be upon them even now.

"Your aunts," he said. "Should I not wait to see if they need help?"

"They never need help," said Sophia.

"But . . ." muttered Srebnitz.

"Not for themselves," she said. "For The Land only."

"But what will they do to them?" asked Srebnitz, as they still walked away.

"Oh, they are very good at talking to Germans," said Sophia. "They have been to our house before."

"What do your aunts say?" he asked.

"They listen to all that the Germans say, first," she said.

"And then?" asked Srebnitz.

"Then they talk about blood," said Sophia. "Pigs' blood, I mean; and all the things you can do with it, and about a sausage called *blut-wurst*. They know all about cooking, and they can talk German."

"And the Germans listen?" he asked.

"On their knees," said Sophia.

And he glanced at her face for fear she was laughing at him. But it was too dark to see.

"One of them asked Aunt Isabella yesterday," Sophia went on, "if she was not highly born. And she said Yes, she was one of the pigs of Swines' Sty. But she said it in our language, which is in any case finer than theirs; and I think they were awed by the sound of it. Anyway, they didn't shoot her, and I don't think they will tonight."

Srebnitz sighed. "But what about you?" he asked.

"I shall go back, when they are gone," she said.

"How will your aunts account for your not being there now?" he asked.

"They may not find out I live there," she said. "There were only two cups on the table. If they do find out, I think Aunt Angelica will explain to them. She is very good at talking the shepherds' dialect, and she can talk it very fast."

All the while they were walking quickly towards the Mountain.

At first there were gardens at the backs of the houses, all the way on their left, and on the right what looked like orchards or orange-groves, but it was now too dark to be sure.

"Have you a box of matches?" asked Srebnitz. "I cannot see your face."

"You saw it in the house," said Sophia.

"That was a long time ago," said Srebnitz.

"Have you no matches?" asked Sophia.

"No," said Srebnitz.

"Hlaka will say something to you, if you come to him without matches," said Sophia.

"What will he say?" asked Srebnitz.

"He will say a great deal," said Sophia.

"Will he be angry?"

"I hope not," Sophia replied.

"Why will he say a great deal?" asked Srebnitz.

"Because he likes his men to have more sense," answered Sophia.

Srebnitz thought a while about that, and realised that Hlaka would be right.

"What is Hlaka like when he is angry?" he asked.

"They say things are bad on the Mountain when Hlaka is angry," she said.

"How long has he been in the Mountain?" asked Srebnitz.

"Over a week," said Sophia. "He went up there when the Germans broke through the line. He was too old to be a regular soldier, and had not fought in this war till he went to the Mountain."

"Has he fought any battles yet?" asked Srebnitz.

"He doesn't fight," said Sophia. "He kills."

That was what Gregor had said.

"In the end he will die fighting," said Sophia. "But he wishes to kill first."

"Has he killed many yet?" asked Srebnitz.

"I don't know," said Sophia. "They say he means to kill two hundred with his own hand before he shows himself much, and that he will be very little seen on the Mountain until he has done that. And that is what he makes all his men do; hardly to kill as many as he does, but not to be seen. Hlaka gets very angry if he hears much firing, because he knows his men have been showing themselves, and he flogs them. Sometimes he goes down into the town. But that is different. He does not go as Hlaka."

"Will you give me a box of matches?" asked Srebnitz, rightly guessing she had some.

"Yes," said Sophia, "if you do not waste them." And he held out his hand. "Not now," said Sophia, "you do not need them yet."

The dark lane led away from the houses now, to the right among fields and orchards. They walked in silence and darkness. Other young men had told of walking with girls along lanes on spring nights such as this, and Srebnitz had thrilled to hear; but instead of stars and fruit-blossoms over their heads, though they were actually there, there seemed something else over both of them: it was the huge wings of Death. He thought of the beauty of Sophia's face, and wanted to see it again, but she would not give him a match. And then, just as he was going to ask again, they saw flashes of light ahead of them, for they were coming back to streets. All the houses were dark, and the flashes were from electric torches carried by Germans. "You cannot come any further," said Srebnitz.

But Sophia said, "You cannot find your way alone. I will turn back when I come to the houses."

They slanted towards their left, and there were the houses, and beyond them the Mountain, visible under the stars. Rubbish-heaps, and tins thrown out from small houses, were about them; and they came to a street, slabs of bare rock at first, and then pavement. A wider street crossed it a little way off, and it was from this that the flashes came, and shone down the side-streets as the Germans came to crossings. Here Sophia, speaking in whispers now, gave Srebnitz the blanket she carried and the matches that he had asked for, and showed him the way: he must cross two more streets after the wide one, and that would bring him to open country, or to country as open as it ever is near a town, wire and market-gardens and very soon a small wood, and then the Mountain.

"Do you think you will be able to see the Mountain?" she asked.

And in the darkness Srebnitz could not be sure whether or not she was laughing at him. So he said that he could see the Mountain now. Then it was time to say good-bye, and Srebnitz stepped on the pavement, pausing for a moment to find all the words of thanks that were due, and to warn Sophia to go quietly and watchfully. But Sophia was gone.

V

FOR a while Srebnitz stood listening, but all was quiet down the lane by which Sophia went. Then he moved without a sound along the little street, and soon came to the edge of the wider street, from which the lights had flashed. He was still in his bare feet. The lights were flashing in the street, both to left and to right of him, and it seemed full of Germans. So he walked across it; and the street to

which he came seemed empty, and it slanted steeply, as
though its pavement were the hem of a cloak that covered
the feet of the Mountain.

There were no sounds ahead of him, yet he walked
warily, for the Germans in the town were uneasy, as the
sounds behind him showed, and he expected them to have
sentries at all the exits, especially towards the Mountain.
He crossed another street safely, but now he heard sounds
of marching behind him, as a patrol turned from the
wider street and up the street he was in. Srebnitz quick-
ened his pace then to a very slow run, but went no faster
than that, in case he should run into a sentry ahead of him.
A sentry was less likely to be out in the road than on the
pavement, but Srebnitz ran on the pavement for the sake of
the ease with which his bare feet could move on its smooth
surface, and the mastery that he felt that his speed could
give him there against any opponent he might meet in the
night; and he felt almost as safe from the marching feet
behind him as a hawk might feel from the feet of a game-
keeper on a night as dark as this. He crossed another
street, the last of them, and still he had met no opposition.
Then he dropped to a walk again; the German patrol was
still behind him, but his only fear now was of a barricade,
or a group of sentries, at the end of the street.

He went very cautiously past the last houses, and then the
pavement ended and there was no sentry there. More than
likely the men marching behind him were the very men
who were to close the end of the street, and he was a few

yards ahead of the news of what he had done. Certainly the patrol came no further than the end of the street.

Very soon the road by which he was travelling was no more than an ordinary country road. He stopped then and listened attentively for as long as he thought it would take Sophia to return to her home, and, hearing no shots, was sure she had got home in safety. Then he looked carefully at both sides of the road to see what sort of obstacles bounded it, and found a hedge on both sides, not too thick for him to get through if he had to.

Then he walked on slowly down the road, and presently the hedges ceased altogether. Then he came to the wood of which Sophia had told him, a pine-wood dark and mysterious in the night, but he felt that with his bare feet and his rifle he was as dangerous as any mystery in the wood. Tall asphodels shone faintly in the light from the stars: nothing else in all the wood gathered any radiance. Srebnitz felt more confidence now than he had felt before in that night, for he felt that if he met anyone now he could use his rifle and still get to the Mountain before he was overtaken; and if the worst should come to the worst, he meant to use it, which would have been impossible in the town, if he was to escape afterwards; and he meant to escape, for he had much to do for The Land. The road ran through the wood and brought him to heathy country without fields. The Mountain rose before him, but the road ran rather to the right than straight upwards. Yet he kept to the road, which seemed to know its business, rather than

go straight up, which seemed so easy; for he had heard of
men who had been lost on the Mountain.

When he was far from the town he sat down and put on
his boots, tying them with many knots, for he had cut the
laces earlier in the night. He put them on, not so much
for protection for his feet on the road, but in case he should
have to take to the rough country. The road had no
boundaries any longer, and he felt almost perfectly safe
now, for any patrol he might meet on the road would never
overtake him in the rough country by night. He had only
to run a few yards to his left, and the night and the Mountain would take care of him.

So he went on slowly through the night, thinking of
Hlaka, and of the victory of The Land, which many doubted
and which the Germans had not even considered as a pos-
sibility, or as an eventuality worthy of the trouble of any
of their speakers to deny, but Srebnitz saw it vividly, and
Hlaka up in the Mountain never saw anything else; for
Srebnitz victory for The Land was a faith, but Hlaka up
in the Mountain with his band of free men saw it all round
him as the saints see Paradise. The eastern stars paled
and a light came low in the sky and the night seemed to
grow colder.

Srebnitz was glad of the second blanket that Sophia had
given him, and that he wore like a cloak. He was too young
to know that sleeplessness and hunger are two other causes
of cold, besides the obvious one of the wind before dawn
on a mountain; but a very elementary instinct prompted him

to eat food, and he sat down by the road and cut a slice
from the ham that Sophia had given him and a slice of
bread from a loaf, both with the knife that had killed the
sentry. The knife reminded him of his fulfilled dream,
the rifle now in his hands, and he raised the rifle to his
lips and kissed it.

Dawn as he ate came up coldly and slowly, first in a
dead hush, then with the familiar sounds that accompany
dawn in Europe, rising up from the far town, the dull and
occasional rap of volleys of musketry. Reprisals already,
thought Srebnitz. A feeling of horror went through him for
a moment. And then he remembered Gregor's words, that
all these people were lost already. Today, tomorrow or
next day they would die: only The Land would be saved.
At a certain altitude above the town Liberty seemed to dwell.
Down below in the streets he was a fugitive, a man without
a permit, and in his father's house he was one of a conquered race; but just about where he was now something in
the feel of the air seemed to tell him there ran the frontier
of Liberty. Near here, or further up where Hlaka served
her, Liberty was enthroned. Her banners were beginning
to show over the Mountain now, as the sun, although not
yet risen, caught floating clouds; and larks rose up to sing
to her. Her palace roof was over his head, the open sky; its
great bastion rose beside him, the wild Mountain. He was
going to join her guards. Then the boy's mind, playing with
fancies, tried to picture what uniform the guards of Liberty
should wear, and fancied them for a moment gorgeous in

gold lace, marching into the capital when victory came. And suddenly a glance, straying from dreams, fell on his own clothes, and he realised that the Guards of Liberty were cloaked with a brown blanket, and wore plain clothes, much like his own, with a red sleeve.

VI

THE fancies had turned to dreams, and Srebnitz, starting up and seeing broad daylight, realised that it was time for him to go on at once, before any patrol should come out from the town. He flung an end of his blanket over one shoulder and stooped to pick up his rifle on his right side, then sprang to his left, spun around and looked all about him, and found his rifle was gone. If an earthquake had sunk the Mountain into the earth, leaving him on the brink, he could not have felt more aghast. Indeed the Mountain seemed lost to him now. For he could not go to Hlaka without a rifle. But then he could not go back to the town, with blood on his sleeve. What could he do? And after a while another question came to him. Why had the German rifle been taken from him, and he been left alive? A man picknicking in an Indian jungle, and falling asleep, scarcely expects his cup of tea to be drunk by a tiger, and himself to be spared. If the cup of tea was drunk, it was not by a tiger. Who then took his rifle? The sun had not risen when he had fallen asleep. It was death to be out without a permit between sunset and sunrise. And it was death to be in possession of arms. And death to rob the German army of anything. And as for his right sleeve . . . ! Was another man going to join Hlaka with his rifle? It was the thought of that that made him turn up the Mountain, still following the road, instead of going the other way. He would go to Hlaka and complain that he had been robbed.

He hurried up the road for nearly an hour. Then, where the last scraps of wild vegetation grew, before scrub and flowers ended in bare mountain, he saw a few thin sheep grazing, and an old shepherd standing near them, not far from the road, in one of the vast coats that the shepherds of those lands wear, made out of many sheep-skins. The shepherd was tall and still powerful, and was looking at Srebnitz with a fixed look, more like a frown.

Srebnitz shouted "Good morning" to him, but the shepherd neither answered nor changed his expression. So Srebnitz went on, but felt uneasily that from those craggy eyebrows he was being frowned upon still.

After that he saw nobody any more, and in another hour he came, in the bare mountain, to the end of the road amongst rocks as large as cottages, lying below a cliff. Tracks wound up from there, but only tracks, and Srebnitz wondered what Gregor had meant, when he had said that he could go to any part of the Mountain and that he would come on Hlaka. He called with the long clear cry, that they use in that land, calling the name of Gregor. And the only answer was echoes.

His despair stimulated in him a feverish energy, and he hurried by one of the steep foot-tracks still higher upward. A few bits of a heath-like plant, or stunted bush, grew about him: the rest of the slope was a shiny crumbled stone. To his right the Mountain rose into peaks, but above him the sky-line was not far away. This he soon reached, and saw before him a flat circular space, scarcely a hundred yards across, with little steep hills all round it. He went down to it by a small pass between two miniature hills, and walked across it, and found that he had come to the top of that part of the Mountain. He called again, but even the echoes seemed less responsive here.

He looked away over the plains that lay to the north of the Mountain, and, the sun having gone behind a cloud, he saw them all shadowed. All Europe is under a shadow, thought Srebnitz; and, finding Nature matched by his mood, drew dark omens from the sombre guise of the view.

He turned round then and walked back to look at the city below him, on the other side, to the south. As he re-crossed the level arena he noticed, this time, in the midst of it a looser patch of sandy soil, a little circle less than a yard across. He went up to look at it and disturbed the loose soil with his foot; as he did so and revealed black cinders beneath, a voice said to him in ordinary conversational tones, "Leave that alone."

He looked up and at first saw no one. Then a young man walked towards him down a rocky slope of the hills that stood round the arena no higher than the houses of a good street. He carried a rifle, and wore a bandolier.

Srebnitz gazed at him in silence, and as he gazed he saw other men come over the rocks all round him. There were about ten of them, men in rough dress like his own; and Srebnitz said to the man that he saw first: "I have come to join Hlaka."

The man walked further towards him before he spoke, and when he spoke he said: "Hlaka does not take everyone."

In desperation then Srebnitz staked his wealth: "I have six loaves of bread," he said, "and a ham and twenty-five cartridges."

In the man's face Srebnitz thought he saw some acknowledgment of the weight of his argument when he mentioned the bread, and almost a slight smile at the fewness of his cartridges. But the man said nothing till he came to the level ground and walked still nearer to Srebnitz and looked at him. Then he said: "Hlaka is angry with you."

"Hlaka?" said Srebnitz. "Why?"

The other men were coming near him too and among them he saw Gregor. His face lit up, but a very slight smile showed on Gregor's, and there was no welcome in any of the faces, as though no smile or welcome could thrive on the Mountain under the anger of Hlaka. Srebnitz opened his sack and drew out the ham and the loaves and said: "I have brought these," and took out the bacon that was hidden under his clothes, and the packets of tea and sugar out of his pockets, and laid them all down beside the loaves and ham on the sack. The eyes of all showed interest. Then Gregor came up to Srebnitz and drew him a little away from the rest and said to him gravely in a low voice: "Why did you not carry your rifle with the stock foremost as I told you?"

Srebnitz said: "It was almost dark. Nobody could see me. I should have remembered as soon as it got light."

Gregor said: "Hlaka can see in the dark."

"I am sorry," said Srebnitz.

"And then," Gregor went on, "you went to sleep. Hlaka never lets any men sleep until they are hidden. And you went to sleep on the road."

"By the side of the road," said Srebnitz.

But Gregor paid no attention. His face was grave, and they walked for a while in silence.

"Who got my rifle?" asked Srebnitz.

"You must ask Hlaka that," said Gregor. "He is Master of the Mountain."

"But how will he know?" asked Srebnitz.

"Nothing goes on in the Mountain that he does not know," answered Gregor.

"What will he do?" asked Srebnitz.

"He is very angry," said Gregor. Then he glanced at Srebnitz's right hand and sleeve. "I'll tell you what," he said; "as soon as you see Hlaka, shake hands with him. He may shake hands with you when he sees your hand like that. And then perhaps . . ."

"But where is Hlaka?" asked Srebnitz.

"I told you," said Gregor. "He is in the Mountain. You only had to come to the Mountain to find him."

"But what part of the Mountain?" asked Srebnitz.

"Here," said Gregor.

And walking down a slope of the little rocky hill, Srebnitz saw the old shepherd, but taller and straighter than he had seemed before, and even fiercer. Like all the others he carried a rifle, and Srebnitz thought he recognized his; at least it had a patch of blood of the same size on the same part of the stock. As Hlaka came to the flat arena Srebnitz walked towards him and stretched out his right hand, as Gregor had advised, towards the frowning figure. Hlaka flashed a fierce glance at him.

"Is that man's blood?" he asked, moving his rifle to his left hand and pointing at Srebnitz's right.

"Yes," said Srebnitz.

"Then I will shake hands with you," said Hlaka, and a grim smile came to his lips.

"May I have my rifle?" asked Srebnitz, emboldened by that smile.

"No," said Hlaka. "You have a man's hand, but a sheep's brains." Then he turned to Gregor and said: "Teach him sense. And he shall have his rifle."

Gregor began at once. "You must not shout on the Mountain," he said. "If you want any of us at any time, light a fire by day and walk away from it as fast as you can down-wind for ten minutes. There is always a wind on the Mountain. And one of us will come to you there, ten

minutes walk down-wind of the fire. If you should want one
of us at night light two fires some yards apart, and the second one, which should be the smaller of the two, will show
the direction in which you went. Walk for a quarter of an
hour at night, and then wait until someone comes to you.
And you must obey orders. I told you to carry your rifle
with the stock forward. Any man unknown to Hlaka, with
a rifle on the Mountain, carrying it any other way is likely
to be shot."

"Did Hlaka take my rifle?" asked Srebnitz.

"Hlaka educates us all," was all that Gregor said.

"Educates?" said Srebnitz, with something in his voice
that seemed to boast that the education he had just absorbed
from the final course of the top class of his school was
something superior to any education that could be possessed
by a rough fierce man like Hlaka.

"Listen," said Gregor. "There is only one study for
Europe now. You had a pen and ink when you went to
school, and masters taught you how to use them, and told
you everything. Now you have your knife and you are
under one of the greatest masters at our end of Europe,
and you know nothing. But you will learn a great deal. You
will learn never to go to sleep where anybody can find you.
You will learn not to shout when the enemy is within hearing. You will learn not to uncover the ashes of fires that
have been hidden. We will teach you hundreds of things.
And when you have learned them you will save The Land
with all of us, and march back to the town when the flag

flies again, or perhaps stand in bronze in the Central Square
for ever. You brought a satchel of good books with you,"
and Gregor pointed to the loaves and ham and packets of tea
and sugar on the sack. "You will learn."

"I brought these cartridges too," said Srebnitz, touching
his bandolier, for his repute seemed to be sunk low and he
wanted to raise it a little.

"Yes," said Gregor. "Tell me how you got them."

And Srebnitz told the story, walking up and down the
flat arena among the miniature peaks. Gregor listened with
the attention of a schoolmaster hearing a boy's lesson.
When Srebnitz had finished he nodded.

"That was all right, wasn't it?" said Srebnitz

"No," said Gregor. "You shouldn't have thrown the
bayonet into that door."

"But why not?" asked Srebnitz.

"You must learn things like that," said Gregor. "It
showed the direction in which you were going. It showed
you were going up that street. And that street leads to the
Mountain."

"But I might have been stopping anywhere on the way,"
said Srebnitz.

"Yes," said Gregor. "You might have been going to have
a cup of tea in any of the houses. But after killing the sentry
the Gestapo would expect you to be leaving the town, and
you showed them the direction in which you would leave it."

"I see," said Srebnitz.

"You must study these things," said Gregor. "There is only one branch of study now for all Europe, and there's no master better than Hlaka. But he is severe."

"I'll try," said Srebnitz.

"What way is the wind blowing?" said Gregor.

"I don't know," replied Srebnitz.

"You must always know from what point the wind is blowing," said Gregor.

A low whistle sounded, and all the men in the little arena began moving outwards towards the rocks.

"There is an aeroplane coming," said Gregor.

"Where is it?" asked Srebnitz.

"We can't see it yet," said Gregor. "We have a listening apparatus. We go to those caves," and he pointed to hollows under ledges of rock where the wild sheep sometimes rested. They were no more than hollows worn by the wind in a softer stratum about three feet deep, under a harder one, and they did not go many feet into the mountain. Gregor began to walk towards one of them, and Srebnitz turned to come with him.

"You mustn't leave your sack and bread lying there," said Gregor.

Srebnitz ran to collect them, while Gregor walked towards the sheltering rock. Srebnitz rejoined him just as he reached it.

"There it comes," said Gregor, pointing to a speck in the sky, and both of them went into the shallow cave. The aeroplane roared over, and went away to the north. When it was out of hearing Srebnitz crawled out, but Gregor told him to wait.

"If he is searching the Mountain," he said, "he will circle back about now."

But no aeroplane returned. It was away on some journey.

"Where is the army?" asked Srebnitz, wondering that the plane had seen nothing.

"Some of them are up among those peaks," said Gregor. Something in his hesitation as he spoke brought into Srebnitz's mind a surprising suspicion.

"Where is the main body?" he asked.

"It is enough for the purpose," said Gregor, "and grows every day."

"Are we the main body?" asked Srebnitz.

Gregor smiled, but said nothing; and later that day Srebnitz learned that the total force in the Mountain was fifteen men. His hopes of being allowed to join the band now increased. Presently Gregor spoke again. "Don't think we are too few," he said. "Every man has two hundred cartridges, and we all use our brains. The Land will be freed, and we shall free it."

And now Hlaka and all his men, for five more had come down the Mountain, were gathered in the midst of the little arena, where the sandy soil had been thrown over the cinders.

"A cloudy day," said Gregor, "we shall have a hot dinner."

Srebnitz, who did not at once see the connection, remained silent. But as soon as a fire was lit he saw, as his imagination had been unable to see, that the surrounding slopes would hide the column of smoke, and that the lighter clouds of it that might stray over the rocks could only be seen against a clear sky.

An armful of dry scrub had made the fire and one of the men stood watching it with bunches of dry grass in his hands, which he put under any twigs that were smoking too much, turning the smoke to flame. A cauldron and a tripod had been brought out of a cave, and in it the cook boiled mutton. A heap was lying on the ground near the fire, which Gregor explained to Srebnitz was a wet blanket ready to throw over the fire if an aeroplane came. There seemed as much to learn in the Mountain as on the day when a boy is first introduced to algebra, or even Euclid, and Gregor explained that the sides of the blanket had all been cut into curves, because nothing in nature is straight and angular, and anything that is stands out at once and catches the eye. And Gregor explained that when the blanket was used men would tread on it to lower its height, and throw a few handfuls of earth on it to break up its colour.

The cook had been, a few days before, the chef in one of the best hotels in the town, which he had left before the Germans came; and, as he found that the manager was preparing to receive German officers, he brought away with him, for better uses, all the pots and pans and knives that he needed for cooking. He was a hearty man, with a plump red face, on which was a merry expression, shadowed, as a bright precipice might be shadowed by the passing wing of an eagle, by one grim purpose. He, like all the rest, had a stubbly chin, on which a beard was growing, all but grey-headed Hlaka, who, perhaps proud of his dark moustache, would allow no white hairs to grow near it, and so shaved; or perhaps he felt that his face was so well known in The Land that to alter the look of it would be like defacing a coin.

All the men cut their meat with the same thin sharp knives that Srebnitz had used to get the rifle that he had now lost. They sat down in a circle round the fire, with Hlaka at the head of the group; that is to say, facing towards the city. Some touch of geniality came into the grim man's features seated there with his men, and, though all of them were given the appearance of brigands by their arms and their clothes, and outlaws by their situation, there was a look in all their faces that went with neither of these things. Nor was that look at all the look of a people of a defeated country; far more they looked like creatures escaped from prison, not criminals, but rather happy sparrows on window-sills outside some place of torment. Never had liberty seemed so precious in that land as it seemed now when it was so rare, and there was none among them who did not feel to the full the luxury of being free. Defeat below them in the town, that lay under the shadow of Hitler, did not prevent them making jokes as they passed round their sweet and resinous wine in bottles of antique pattern. Whatever the past had been, the present was merry, and the future, for them, was radiant.

Srebnitz, although not yet permitted a rifle, was allowed the friendship of these men, and soon they heard from him how his parents had been slaughtered. Hlaka looked up, at that, and asked suddenly for the name of the Prussian major of whom Srebnitz had told, the man who had found the attitude of his mother incorrect. Srebnitz had found out the major's name before he had left his home, while the Prussian slept in a chair: it was Major von Wald, and this he told. And Hlaka said to a man beside him: "Bring me the book."

And this man went away to one of the many hollows between ledge and ledge of rock, and brought a book in a binding of rough leather, while another man brought him a pen and ink. And Hlaka took the pen, made of an eagle's feather, and dipped it into the ink and said to Srebnitz: "It is death for any man to have his name in this book."

Then he threw a pinch of sand over the name that he had written, and gave one of his men the book to return to its safe place.

The clouds that had been gathering in the morning grew blacker during the meal, and before it was ended there fell one of those showers that fill for a few hours the water-courses of the Mountain, that are often dry for weeks, except for a few pools that lie in the deeper hollows, and keep alive butterflies and wandering men, and wild sheep and more other lives than one knows of. It came down suddenly from the clouds to the north, and helped that small band of free men to quench their fire, and washed Srebnitz's right hand clean. Two men removed the cauldron and its tripod, the cook went away with his pots and pans, while others threw wet sand over the cinders and all of them went for shelter into their shallow caves. And soon there was no sign of men in the Mountain, or that any free men were living in all The Land.

VII

IN THE small cave, sheltering from the rain, Srebnitz's lessons continued. Gregor explained to him that there were five thousand Germans in the town, and that one by one these must be killed. The first thing, he said, was not to show yourself, and he showed him how to hide in front of things as well as behind things, and taught him to know where the horizon would be to any watcher below, so that he should never come between a German's eyes and the sky. He told him about the oak-scrub, the heath and the myrtle, and the various kinds of cover. And he must never fire a shot at a hundred yards. Hlaka might sometimes fire at two hundred, he said; but no one else was allowed to fire at a hundred. Infantry sometimes fired at a thousand yards, said Gregor; but that was in war, and in war it took a ton of lead to kill a man. This was guerrilla; and they had not a ton to spare. If they never wasted a cartridge and never showed themselves, they would kill the Germans in time. "But won't the Germans do the same thing and kill us?" said Srebnitz. "And they are two or three hundred to one."

"No," said Gregor. "They have not the brains for it. Very fine plans are worked out for them, by men well capable of working out plans. There are no better plans in the world. And they have worked them out for years, while we were all sleeping. And there are no better men to obey those plans than Germans."

"Then why won't they work?" asked Srebnitz.

"They do work," said Gregor. "They broke the Maginot Line and conquered Europe, and have taken all The Land except this Mountain. They were brilliant plans, well carried out. But they made no plan for fighting in oak-scrub on a mountain. And it's too late now."

"Why is it too late?" asked Srebnitz.

"I don't quite know," said Gregor. "But all the plans were made years ago, when Hitler was speaking of peace, and they have to follow those plans now. Everything they have done was foreseen. And we of course, who foresaw nothing, we lost where they won. But where they did not foresee, there are no plans; and without plans Germans can do nothing. They foresaw everything for two years, but the two years are running to an end, and the plans go no further. Soon they will be like children lost in the dark. Hlaka will make his plans from hour to hour; but they will ask their great generals for plans, and the generals will look among their papers and not find any more."

"And can we fight five thousand men?" asked Srebnitz.

"Why not?" said Gregor. "Five thousand men can't kill a coney. Some men are born hunters; the Germans are born plotters. Good plotters too. But we are hunters."

"We shall win, then," said Srebnitz, but a little doubtfully.

"Certainly we shall win," said Gregor. "But you must obey Hlaka."

Then Gregor picked up the little air-gun that was in the cave and gave Srebnitz a small spade and told him to come and practise some shooting.

"But I can shoot from here," said Srebnitz.

"No," said Gregor. "We never shoot till we are hidden."

"But I am hidden here," said Srebnitz.

"No," said Gregor. "That is too easy. You cannot always go to a cave when you want to shoot. You must learn how to hide yourself on the Mountain, wherever you are."

"What is the spade for?" asked Srebnitz, as they walked out of the cave.

"We all carry spades or trowels," said Gregor. "It is often necessary in order to hide ourselves. And we are not allowed to shoot until we have done that."

Gregor led the way out by the back of the arena through the rocks to the north, stooping and crawling when he came to the top of the crags. Then they came round to their left and walked down the bare slope on the south side, facing the town.

"Can't they see us here?" asked Srebnitz.

"Hlaka wants us to be seen a bit on the Mountain today," Gregor replied. And they went on till they came to the heath and the patches of oak-scrub. There he told Srebnitz to hide himself.

"Where?" asked Srebnitz.

"Anywhere," answered Gregor.

And Srebnitz lay down behind a tuft of heath and took the air-gun from Gregor. Then Gregor went with a match-box and set it up on a stone at seventy paces, lower down the slope. Then he walked back to Srebnitz.

"I can see you clearly from there," he said. "Only your head and shoulders are hidden."

And he made Srebnitz dig so as to sink himself a little, and made him dig up two more plants of heath, and hide the scar where he had dug them up, and showed him how to arrange them. Then he went back to within two or three yards of the match-box and looked towards Srebnitz and, when he was satisfied that he could not be seen from that point by a man standing up, he made a signal to Srebnitz. And Srebnitz began shooting. And Gregor corrected his aim after every shot. Srebnitz shot about forty pellets, and Gregor was pleased with his shooting.

"All you have to do now," he said, "is to learn to hide yourself."

"I am afraid it was only with an air-gun," said Srebnitz, feeling that some little depreciation was due after Gregor's praise.

"An air-gun is the next best thing after a military rifle," said Gregor, "because the back-sight is dark. No sporting rifles are any good, because the back-sights are shiny. The gunmakers make them shiny with thin strips of silver. No-one can see a bright foresight properly over a shining back-sight. But our rifles are all military rifles, and they are all right."

Then they walked back to the little arena which, with the caves in the rocks near it, was more their home than any other part of the Mountain.

It was still raining as they went into their cave; but Gregor explained to Srebnitz that they took no notice of rain, because, as it was said among the shepherds and as Hlaka's men appeared to find it, ill-health was impossible on the Mountain; but in spite of this, he said, they always slept in dry clothes, and would all dry their clothes before a good fire that night.

Hlaka had been walking about, watching the clouds, and before evening they cleared away from the sun, rolling southwards in great splendour, and Hlaka began to send a message by helio down to the town.

"What is he signalling?" asked Srebnitz.

"He signals names of German officers that are in that book," said Gregor. "He would be sending the name of Major von Wald now."

Three times Hlaka signalled, to different parts of the town.

"Has he signalled his address?" asked Srebnitz, for the twinkling flashes seemed too few for that.

"No," said Gregor, "he sends no addresses. They will know where to find him down there."

"What code does he use?" ask Srebnitz.

"No code," replied Gregor. "Just the name in plain Morse."

"Will they not take precautions?" asked Srebnitz.

"Yes," said Gregor. "They will take many precautions. They are no use against us."

And Srebnitz began to feel from that moment that there was some strange power in Hlaka, with his little band on the Mountain, which must not be measured merely by such numbers as fifteen and five thousand; a power that dared in its infancy to challenge the might of Germany, a growing power of which hope whispered that it might one day free The Land.

He had not helioed from near the caves, but from the ridge of the Mountain further along to the west. When he returned to his cave one of the men came with a message to Gregor, and Gregor told Srebnitz that they would march just before dark to another part of the Mountain. He explained that other armies fall in before they march, and stand for some time on parade, but that Hlaka's men did the opposite and scattered and would all meet Hlaka as darkness fell, at the point he had named. The stormy clouds of sunset all turned to gold, and Hlaka's men saw in them a prophetic glory. The Germans in the town saw the same golden splendour; but, if they had augurs among them who could read the future, they surely read a menace in that sunset, that to the men on the Mountain boded only glory.

VIII

BIRDS passed over the Mountain into silence and twilight, and Hlaka's men one by one stole out from their caves, and moved a little way westwards and disappeared. All knew where the meeting-place was to be except Srebnitz, and Gregor went with him. A star came out as they went, and very soon day was hidden by the western end of the Mountain. They were moving through heath near to the line where it ended on the bare rocks of the Mountain. They were walking in some sort of track that Srebnitz could scarcely see, among the dark plants of the heath, and he followed Gregor till Gregor was only a dark shape in the night, and they came to the meeting-place and found Hlaka standing there with some of his men beside him. And the rest came quietly up, shape by shape appearing suddenly out of the darkness. All had armfuls of wood, and these they threw down before Hlaka, and handfuls of straw were brought and set alight, and soon a great cluster of flames was dancing there on the Mountain. The men took their coats off and held them to dry at the fire. Srebnitz glanced in the direction of the town, for, though they were near the top of the ridge, they were on the southern side of it, towards the west, and in full view of the streets.

"Why does he not light his fire on the other side of the Mountain?" asked Srebnitz.

"That is Hlaka's affair," said Gregor.

And he turned towards the fire, where the cook was already getting to work with his frying-pan, and Srebnitz followed. The men sat down, not in a circle round the fire, but in a semi-circle facing the west, all but one man who stood watching. It was slices of ham that the cook was frying, and they were very soon ready and were handed round quickly on tin plates. When the slices of ham were eaten, one bottle of wine was sent round. Then a gourd-like instrument with strings was brought out by a man called Iskander, and he played a few bars with a bow and was about to sing, when the man on watch shouted "Flash!"

They got up quickly then, and two men helped the cook and they walked away from the fire with everything that they had, back in the direction from which they had come.

Then they heard the boom of a gun and its echoes wandering away, roaming up little valleys that twisted into the Mountain, and coming at last to the peaks, and running along them awhile from rock to rock, and falling back into silence. Then they heard the sound of a shell, that had gone up from the town into the night sky, coming down towards them and humming as it came. It fell nearly two hundred yards short of the fire and burst, and its fragments flew over the Mountain, crying with that wild scream that man has let loose amongst man, not having sufficient wild beasts with which to tear his enemies. And when the last of the echoes from this shell had fallen from peak and cliff, like dead mountaineers into the darkness and silence, Srebnitz saw the flash of another shot in the town.

Then men who had lain down when they heard the first shell coming got up now and walked still further away from the fire and lay down again when they heard the snarl of the second shell, which burst far over the fire near the top of the ridge. Again they went on, and Srebnitz saw a third flash, and heard the boom of the cannon again send its echoes all over the Mountain; and the third shell lit in the very midst of the fire, sending up with most graceful curves a fountain of ruby and gold; and Hlaka's men all cheered, for they loved good shooting.

Then they all went back to the caves in which they used to sleep.

"Hlaka wants them to see something of us up here," Gregor explained to Srebnitz, "because he wants more rifles."

Srebnitz, who was learning the ways of the Mountain was beginning to understand. "They will come up to look for us?" he said.

"Yes," said Gregor. "They will come."

"Will Hlaka let me have my rifle?" asked Srebnitz.

"All rifles on this mountain are his rifles," said Gregor. "But I will tell him that you shot straight at seventy yards, and he may let you have it tomorrow."

"Will they come tomorrow?" Srebnitz asked.

"Yes," said Gregor, "they are certain to come tomorrow. And we shall get some more rifles."

It was as warm as our summer, down on the plain, but spring climbed the Mountain slowly, and almost stumbled at night; so that in the shallow caves that the wild sheep knew, it was little warmer in April than are the gusts and smiles of an April morning in England.

Srebnitz learned then that the cold of the night comes as much from below as from above, or from left and right, and Gregor told him not to lay his blankets over him, but to wrap each one round him. This Gregor taught, as elsewhere, in other times, it is taught what $(a+b)$ multiplied by $(a-b)$ amounts to, and Srebnitz learned as boys learn such elementary things, never to be forgotten afterwards, but needing no correction from any master, for the things themselves taught him; as though $a+b$ should rise up from the paper and roughly show their ways, while $a-b$ jostled close to insist on their different lore. But, besides blankets, Srebnitz had a mattress more than a foot thick, made out of heath and coarse grass, which all the men used for beds, and which was not only a protection against the hardness of the mountain, but against some of the cold.

Winds that wander at night and whisper to grasses, dogs barking far off, the voices of night-birds hunting, and all the other sounds that keep awake the dwellers in houses in their first night under the stars, failed to keep Srebnitz for many minutes this side of the border of dreamland. For a little while he felt the discomforts of being without a bed, or warmth, or adequate shelter, and felt their novelty and rejoiced in it; then his own sense of freedom from all the rules and orderly ways of man, which the winds and the mountain nurtured, grew into something grander, and he thought of the freedom of the people of The Land, which he had gone to the Mountain to aid, and this thought grew in splendour, until over the border of dreamland it shone among other dreams.

IX

GREGOR and Srebnitz were in the same cave, and early in the night they were joined by a man who had been on watch; but nothing disturbed Srebnitz until the daylight streamed in and the song of a bird woke him. Or so it seemed to Srebnitz; but there was a stir in the little encampment, and a certain anticipation that all were feeling was perhaps thrilling the air and somehow calling Srebnitz away from dreams. Then Gregor, who was already up and about, stooped down and shouted into the cave to tell Srebnitz that breakfast was ready, and Srebnitz came out and walked with him over the little arena to the place where the fire was burning, and the cook already frying rashers of bacon, and Hlaka and most of his men sat by the fire. Srebnitz, full of zeal for the new life he was living, and eager to know as much of it as he could, asked Gregor as they walked what they would do that morning.

"We have breakfast first," said Gregor.

But they were already within sound of the sizzling of the bacon, and Srebnitz wanted to know more.

"But after that?" asked Srebnitz.

"After that," said Gregor, "we shall go down to the heath and myrtle. The Germans are coming."

"The Germans!" repeated Srebnitz.

And Hlaka, seated beside the fire facing towards the city, and having heard their words, shouted to Srebnitz: "They saw our fire last night. It was very observant of them. They could not see the fire in the hearts of free men. But they saw our fire on the Mountain. They hit it with their gun, so they are not quite blind. But they are coming nearer to look."

And then Srebnitz blurted out, without even thinking, the words that were nearest his heart: "Can I have my rifle?"

"Your rifle?" said Hlaka thoughtfully. And after a while he said, "Yes. If you can take it from me while I am asleep."

"I shall never find you asleep," said Srebnitz, sighing.

And that somehow pleased Hlaka. "No," he said gravely, and added: "Take your rifle," and handed it to Srebnitz, for it was by his side. "And you may have the cartridges in your bandolier," he went on. "But if you waste more than five of them, you will never be given any more." And Hlaka turned to finish his breakfast.

Srcbnitz gathered from the talk of the men round the fire that an aeroplane had come over earlier, without waking him, and had carefully searched the Mountain; and that afterwards about fifty men had been seen on the march, coming away from the town, but were now lost to sight. Sometimes he listened to the talk by the fire about what was going to happen. Sometimes he turned adoring eyes on his rifle.

The bacon was eaten and coffee passed round, coffee with gritty sediment an inch or two deep at the bottom of the tin mugs, better than any coffee that Srebnitz had ever tasted yet; and while the men drank it Hlaka explained what they had to do: the Germans, he said, would come by the only road, with scouts out in front; if they had scouts on each side as well, walking through the oak-scrub and myrtle and heath, the movement of their whole force would be so slow that they would be easily dealt with, but they would not have the patience for this and they would all go by the road; where the slope rose steeply from the roadside Iskander would wait for them, about seventy yards back amongst the myrtle, and would get as many as he could; if they attacked him straight up the mountain, he would retire before them from bush to bush and shoot many more as he went; but they would have more sense than that and would come round on his left or right, and so they would meet another of Hlaka's men, also hidden; and, as they tried to close with him, they would meet another. Seven of the men would be disposed like that, and Hlaka would be with the rest beside the road, much lower down the Mountain, waiting for what remained of the German party. Then his eye fell on Srebnitz: "You can go with Iskander," he said. "And if you show yourself, you're no good to me, and the Germans can have you."

Then they marched off. That is to say they scattered from round the fire, and each man soon disappeared from the sight of anyone that might be watching the Mountain. The Germans, as Hlaka's men left their fire and their breakfast, were coming out of the pine-wood through which Srebnitz had come. Iskander and all the rest were over the ridge on the north side of the Mountain, moving westwards, till they came to little valleys or clefts along which they could move unseen, and went down them on the side that the Germans were. After crossing the ridge with Iskander, Srebnitz saw no more of any of the others. They went where a small stream was running, refreshed by recent rain, and where trees grew two or three times the height of a man, as they grew nowhere else on the upper mountain. Iskander had brought his stringed instrument with him, rather than trust it in a cave near the fire, where the Germans might find it and break it, for the fire had been left burning to guide them up the Mountain, past where Hlaka's men would be waiting for them. He played the instrument as they went through the wood, and sang to it softly, singing old songs of The

Land. As they came out of the wood on to a slope of myrtle and heath they saw the whole length of the road below them. "There they are," said Iskander. And they saw the Germans marching, with three scouts out in front, all on the road.

Srebnitz unslung his rifle and gripped it and moved his finger towards the trigger. Iskander stopped his playing.

"If Hlaka ever sees you do that he will have you flogged," he said.

Srebnitz removed his finger hastily from the trigger.

"Nobody ever does that," said Iskander, "except actually to fire a shot, or to be photographed. We are not being photographed today, and the Germans are two miles off. So don't be silly."

Srebnitz was stung by Iskander's words, and still more deeply abashed by his own stupidity, but he was learning all the time. And Iskander with his rifle still slung from his shoulder went on playing the tunes which in remote summer evenings had grown up in The Land, though now he sang no longer. They went down the slope till they were close to the road, to which the hill plunged steeply. They only had to stoop slightly to be hidden from the road by the slope of the ground. There they stopped, and first Iskander made Srebnitz hide himself, choosing his own tuft of heath; and this Srebnitz did, making use of all that he had learned from Gregor the day before. Iskander crawled lower down and looked at him, and was satisfied, and then found a place for himself a few yards away and unslung his rifle and lay down. Directly below them they could not see the road, for the hill took a steeper plunge within thirty yards of it, but a little to the right of that point they had a perfect view of fifty or sixty yards of road, until a hump of the hill hid it; to their left they could see no more of it, for it curved left-handed on its way up, behind the slope of the hill. Iskander still strummed with his fingers on the wires that ran over his gourd; a martial air, as Srebnitz tried to think, but it was only some rustic song, fallen on Iskander's memory from the history of a free people. He sang no longer, or, if he did, the song was inaudible to Srebnitz only a few yards away.

"Who will shoot first?" asked Srebnitz in a low voice.

"Who ever gets a good bead first on a German," Iskander replied. "But let the scouts go by."

After that they spoke no more. Sometimes Iskander stood up and peered over the heath, and lay down again. After about the fifth time that he did this he made a sign to Srebnitz, and lay quite still. Srebnitz watched the road intently where it curved out of sight a hundred yards away. Then he heard the boots of men marching, and very soon after that two men came into view. Srebnitz never moved, and the men marched on. As they went out of sight below him another man came round the bend and, when he disappeared after the other two, the tramp of boots became louder.

And then the German column came into sight, marching in threes. The leading men were only a hundred yards away, and Srebnitz was about to clutch at the trigger again, when he remembered Iskander's scorn. Then he got the bead of his rifle on the Germans and felt sure that he could not miss, because they were all bunched together, but remembered his orders not to fire at over seventy yards, and knew that he would be judged by what he did now, and dared not disobey. The men marched on, and he kept his sights on them till they seemed to be at about seventy yards; then, being certain of his aim, he fired, and fired a second shot as fast as he could. He did not hear Iskander's shot, because he fired at the same moment.

The Germans at once left the road and got into the heath below it, Iskander firing his second shot as they went; and three men were left lying on the road. Stooping amongst the myrtle, which partly hid them, some of the Germans went back the way they had come, and Iskander shot one of them; others went on in the direction in which they had been going, near to the road, but stooping amongst the myrtle and oak-scrub; and a few remained below Iskander and Srebnitz, shooting at where they supposed them to be, but they were out of sight of the two, and therefore out of shot.

Presently Iskander crawled forward, going through the heath like a snake; and after a while he fired one shot, and then crawled back to Srebnitz. Srebnitz heard for the first time the intensely sharp crack of bullets crashing through air; but they were quite harmless, because he and Iskander were behind the skyline of the men who were shooting towards them. Iskander explained that they were coming round them on both sides up the slope, and that he and Srebnitz, who could no longer see any Germans below them, would move further up the hill.

"Did you get him?" asked Srebnitz.

Iskander nodded his head, and led the way up the hill, still unseen by the Germans. Then, hearing a shot from the men that were now on their right, and then two more, Iskander turned in their direction, and Srebnitz followed, both stooping among the bushes of myrtle. But they had not gone far in that direction when they heard a machine-gun, if not two, turned on to the slope below them, from which the Germans were attacking the centre of the little line of men, the centre which had been Iskander and Srebnitz, but was now only myrtle and heath. So Iskander led Srebnitz more to their left, till they got to a point on the Mountain that was straight above where they had fired their first shots, and Iskander told Srebnitz to get cover here.

"They will come straight up the slope," he said, "after they have finished with their machine-guns. That is their way."

Then he got cover for himself, facing down the slope. There were clearly two machine-guns now, and the ricochets screamed over their heads, and occasionally a stream of crashing cracks of bullets that had hit nothing. There were three or four more shots on what was now their left, and the sound of a shot came from their right, and then another and then a third. In miniature the Germans were doing a pincer movement, and the shots on the right and the left were from Hlaka's men, every one of them fired from close, and no bullets wasted. The copious fire of the machine-guns ceased, and the silence was broken only by two more shots on the left and two on the right; and presently a head appeared over the heath, coming up the slope, and a line of ten men appeared.

"Wait," said Iskander. And Srebnitz waited until he was sure the men were within seventy yards. Then he shot a German through the chest, and fired quickly at another and missed, while Iskander killed one.

"Don't waste bullets," said Iskander in a low voice.

Srebnitz remembered that he had wasted one himself down by the road, yet Iskander's warning steadied him.

Still the Germans had not seen them, and the shots that they fired were no guide to them, because at those close ranges the rifle cannot be heard, but only the crash of the bullet. They were coming slowly up the steep slope, and Srebnitz shot another, and Iskander shot one more also. There were no longer any Germans straight in front of them, and the six survivors at the left end of the German line went on doggedly up the slope. One came close enough to have seen them for certain when he came past the myrtle bush behind which Iskander was, but Iskander shot him, and the rest went on. Soon they were out of sight to Iskander and Srebnitz, lying down in the heath, and Srebnitz raised his head over a flowering shrub, but Iskander signed to him to lie down again, and crawled up to him.

"They'll get above our men and shoot down at them," he said. Then he led Srebnitz stooping through the heath, till they were exactly below the five men that had gone up the mountain.

There they got cover again, and Iskander began to sing an old martial air of his country. He sang it loudly this time, accompanying his song with the music of his strange instrument. The five men halted then, and turned round and listened. Iskander ceased singing, and the men came back down the hill.

Still there were shots from both the left and the right. The Germans' bayonets were fixed, and they came quicker down the slope than they had gone up, and Srebnitz was wondering if they would stop them in time. Just as he wondered, Iskander shot one, who fell with his rifle crashing on to a rock, and his uncouth helmet rolled for a space down the hill. Srebnitz shot another; and at that moment the Germans saw them, and all three came for them, leaping down the hill. But two men passing between two obstacles, a rock and a stunted oak, came for a moment so close to each other that they made one target, and Srebnitz was able to fire a quick shot without fear of missing, and one of the men dropped. And now it was bayonet against rifle, two men against two.

The Germans could not stop to fire, because by the time they steadied themselves and shot they would have made a stationary target for too long; so they rushed on down the hill and came to within a few yards, and Iskander and Srebnitz both fired before the bayonets could reach them. Iskander and Srebnitz had now shot fifteen men. If the three on their left and the three on their right had done as well, there would be few Germans left.

Iskander and Srebnitz started towards what may be called
the right flank, if a line of eight men may be thought large
enough to have flanks. But now the firing ceased and the
Germans were drawing off down the hill, out of range of
men who were forbidden to fire at over a hundred yards.

Iskander then ran down the slope, calling to Srebnitz to
follow, to the place from which they had fired their first
shots, for there were three rifles lying on the road, and a
sudden fear came to Iskander that the retreating Germans
that had gone further up the Mountain would pick up this
valued treasure. But these Germans went wide of the road
through the scrub below, with a big enough detour to avoid
any more losses. Soon all that were left of them were on the
road again and there was no way of overtaking them except
by following down the road, where Hlaka's men must have
been seen, which was forbidden by Hlaka; for the going was
far too rough over the heath and rocks for any men going
that way to keep pace with men on the road. But Hlaka's
eight men, including himself, were in line down below, hidden on each side of the road, waiting.

As soon as the Germans were out of sight Srebnitz ran
up the slope to gather the treasure of ten rifles, and hundreds of rounds of ammunition, while Iskander went down
to the road to get the three rifles there and two more below it.

The firing had been so close that all the Germans that
Srebnitz saw were either dead or dying except one of the
two men that had bunched together, who had made so easy a
shot that Srebnitz had nearly missed through feeling too

sure. This man was shot through the side of the ribs, but not fatally, and was lying on the heath, with his rifle near him. He stretched out his hand for it as Srebnitz came up, but was just unable to reach it. Srebnitz moved the rifle further away, and then put his handkerchief in a wad over one of the wounds to check the bleeding. He did this with one hand, because he could not trust the German enough to put down his rifle. His first aid was therefore slow, and he had not finished when Iskander came up, and looked at him with a certain toleration, but did not help. When Iskander was there Srebnitz put down his rifle, out of reach of the German, and checked the bleeding more easily.

"Hlaka won't have prisoners, you know," said Iskander. "Nor will they."

But Srebnitz went on till he had got the wad of his handkerchief to stay in its place, tied there by the German's handkerchief.

"Can you walk?" asked Srebnitz.

The German nodded.

"Then make off," Srebnitz said.

And the German walked slowly away. Iskander watched him go in silence, till he came to the road, and turned to the right to go back the way by which he had come. "Tell him," said Iskander to Srebnitz then, "that it doesn't matter, but if he goes that way he will be shot."

So Srebnitz ran after the German and explained as well as he could, mostly by signs, that he had better make his way through the open heath. And very soon after that, there came to add a point to what Srebnitz said the sound of firing from Hlaka and the men with him; almost a volley at first, then eight separate shots, then a little more firing, then silence. The German walked slowly away through the rough country downhill. He had not spoken as yet. Then when he had gone about twenty yards some thought seemed to strike him, and he stopped for a moment in meditation. Then he looked over his shoulder at Srebnitz and said in German the one word "Thanks," and went on his way.

Srebnitz returned to Iskander, who smiled as though at some childish prank, unwise but forgivable, and they started to hide a few of their fifteen new rifles and part of the ammunition, and to carry the rest of their booty up to the caves.

The three men who had been on their left were there before them and, one of these being the cook, the fire was lighted and dinner being prepared. Iskander and this little group of three asked each other how many rifles they had got, and the three greeted Srebnitz, but not much was said and there was little rejoicing.

The men were thoughtful, as the magnitude of their task for the first time seemed to come down on them. Fifteen men, escaped from the disaster that had overwhelmed all the rest of their countrymen and was inflicting on hundreds of thousands a form of slavery and tempting five or six of the weaker ones to treachery, fifteen men not only escaped from disaster, but free all of a sudden from the laws and rules that there must always be wherever there is pavement, to lead a life whose cold and hunger and all other hardships invariably charm all men that have known it, fifteen men bound by a new chain of friendship stronger than any they had known before, led by a man they loved, though he sometimes flogged them; these men had been merry at first, rejoicing in the novelties of each day and in their abundant freedom. But now, with all this wealth of new weapons, each man perceived that freedom was not a light and lovely thing to be merely enjoyed by himself, but that it was something vast, like a colossal statue of gold, to be carried laboriously amongst many men, to be set up in the midst of the capital. This, a thing to be dreamed of always, was not a thing to be practically thought of while they had only fifteen rifles; but now, when they knew they must have something like sixty, theirs seemed a poor and trivial force with which to hope to free a country from the armies of a predatory empire.

Three more men came to the camp-fire and, after a few questions and hearty greetings, they too were grave and thoughtful.

And then Hlaka arrived, but not with all his men: his rule that no man was to show himself was simple enough, and he enforced it with as much discipline as that which elsewhere runs to waste in teaching men to clean buttons until they flash; and the Mountain was kind to Hlaka's rule, but mountains are not easily tamed, and no such rules work always, and two of his men had been seen and shot through the head.

Hlaka walked silently to the fire, with no change in the

expression of his face since he had gone down the mountain. Then his eye fell on Srebnitz.

"How many rifles?" he asked.

"Fifteen between us," said Srebnitz, pointing to Iskander.

"How many cartridges did you waste?" asked Hlaka.

"Two between us," said Srebnitz.

Then the expression changed in the rugged face round the eyes, with a change such as spring makes on that mountain when the north wind drops overnight, and Hlaka smiled.

X

THEY sat by a small fire eating their dinner, the survivors of Hlaka's men, a fire mostly of little twigs and coarse grass, because the sky was too clear for them to risk much smoke. They had taken forty-five rifles and two machine-guns and about nine thousand cartridges.

Hlaka made Srebnitz a full member of the band of Liberators, as he called them, raising his hand and blessing his rifle in the name of The Land. "And I make you," he added, "in the name of The Land, what all these men are also, the commander of four thousand men. We have not the men yet, but our hopes know them. They will come to us out of the future, and you shall command them when they come. They are there where our hopes see them and are there till our hopes fail, which will be never."

After that he spoke no more. And all the others talked

of the fight, while Hlaka sat still and silent, like a grey mountain rock.

A little way off on the slope one of Hlaka's men handled the mirror of a helio; far down below there rose, above the dark tops of the pine-trees around it, the tiled dome of a church, a miniature of the church of San Sophia in Istanbul, and on one of its dark windows facing towards the Mountain a speck of light was wavering and dancing. No Morse was used this time; just the speck of borrowed sunlight on the stained glass, hovering there for five minutes.

And in a few more minutes a Bishop of the Orthodox Eastern Church walked out of the grove and garden about the church on to the pavement of a street of the capital, and walked through the town towards the west and the north. He wore a tall black hat with no brim, and a long black cassock, and a gold cross on his chest, suspended from his neck by a chain, and he carried a long black stick with a gold top to it. He had a silken black beard, and a most serene face. He walked calmly right through the town, and no German stopped him. All that he did was as calm as dawn or sunset.

He passed the gate where Srebnitz had killed the sentry; he went out by the same end of the town and walked through the pine-wood; and before the sun was low, Hlaka's men saw him, a solitary figure, dark against the road and small in the distance, coming up the Mountain. Still he kept the same pace, walking without hurry on the flat, and without fatigue on the Mountain.

Two aeroplanes roared all along the slope, flying low, like a pair of birds of prey looking for field-mice, and Hlaka's men hid. The Bishop continued his slow promenade. The aeroplanes disappeared, and Hlaka's men came out again; and Hlaka sent eight of them down the road to escort the Bishop to his headquarters. They escorted him rather as dogs usually escort their master on a walk in the country, that is to say they ran through the myrtle and heath on each side of him. But, though the Bishop seldom saw them from the road where he walked, he perceived their intention, which was to do him honour.

And so he came at length to the little arena among the circle of small crags. And Hlaka bowed to him and told him that two of the Liberators of The Land, as they should be known hereafter, were dead, and that he had sent the signal that had brought the Bishop, in order that they should be buried with such honour as was due to the fame they should have in the years to be.

The two graves were already dug, just over the little crags on the slope that looked to the city; and there the Bishop intoned the burial service of the Church of the East, while Hlaka's men stood near, but behind the crags, so that they were unseen from the streets below. Then the simple graves were filled in, with a rough stone at the head of each, on which a name was scratched with a knife. But nothing was simple about the graves to Hlaka; for, though he lived and worked and thought actively in the present, his dreams all dwelt with the future, in which he vividly saw the whole Land free, and two sepulchres of marble on the Mountain facing towards the city.

And in that perpetual vision of Hlaka's it is probable that the two men now in their graves appeared as immortal legendary figures, almost made visible by a line of the burial service, with which his thoughts were now echoing, "And everlasting be their memory."

Then to the Bishop after his long walk Hlaka offered the hospitality of the Mountain, which was food and drink served to him by the mountaineers on a great chair made out of many coats, whose back was a rock draped with more of them; but to Hlaka it was not so much the Mountain to which he invited the Bishop, but to the free Land of which he knew that he would one day be the Liberator. For as something more than a leader of fourteen men living in a few caves he appeared to receive the Bishop, and the Bishop gravely accepted this grander welcome. He would have rested awhile in the great chair which Hlaka's men had made for him; but Hlaka, who never stayed in one place long, was anxious that the Bishop should be safely away before the Germans did whatever they might do next.

The Bishop felt Hlaka's anxiety, and soon rose and blessed the men, and walked over the rocks to the road, where Hlaka bowed his farewell to him, bareheaded, and the Bishop raised his hand and blessed him and turned for home. And, as he turned, Hlaka said to him: "I have rifles for forty-nine more men."

The Bishop nodded his head, and walked home down the mountain road.

With the Bishop his escort went as far as the pine-wood,

keeping level with him through scrub-oak and myrtle as he
went down the road. One of the escort was Srebnitz. At the
edge of the pine-wood, where the others stopped and lay
behind bushes and watched, Srebnitz ran up to the Bishop
to ask him about the safety of Sophia. The Bishop did not
know her by name and Srebnitz described her, graceful,
bright-eyed, illuminated by her own youth and by Srebnitz's
own vision of her, which made a different picture from what
any other man had seen, as all artists' portraits of the same
face differ, but it conveyed some picture to the Bishop, a
picture of a very young girl, so that he was able to say to
Srebnitz: "She is safe. No girl under twenty was killed this
morning or yesterday."

Evening was descending upon the Mountain as Srebnitz
and the rest of the Bishop's escort returned to the rocky
peaks, and the chill came that is the forerunner of night.
The sun had long disappeared from them, though it was not
yet set over the plains, which still shone with the level rays on
the north side of the mountain. Golden lights began to
twinkle from far-off windows, and Hlaka's men took note
that some new regulation permitted this in the town.

Then the sun set, as they could tell by the smile that went
out of the countryside spread far below them; and at that
moment the German bombers came. Force of habit probably
sent them just at sunset, as it was a favorite time of theirs in
which to attack, and so they came now, though there was no
reason to choose this particular time to attack men who had

no guns. They came, twenty of them, sweeping along the ridge and bombing the heath and myrtle on the south side of it. And Srebnitz heard that sound that German culture and the genius of Hitler have made so familiar to all Europe that it scarcely need be described, the long whining scream and the blow that jarred the earth, and all living and inanimate things within hundreds of yards. Suffice it that Hlaka's men felt the swiftly repeated blows that shook air and earth all round them, and heard the grey mountain peaks repeat meditatively, from peak to peak into distance, this clamour of man, that engaged their august attention, as no murmur of his had ever done before.

XI

THE German squadron of bombers did no harm whatever, unless for some slight scars on the face of the Mountain, that may attract the curiosity of future geologists. The Germans had suffered defeat on the Mountain, and had struck the Mountain in revenge, and to some extent were satisfied. They must have seen with their glasses some slight stir where the funeral had been, for those of Hlaka's men to whom the bombs fell nearest were the two that were dead.

Srebnitz, and even the more experienced Gregor, thought that there would be no fire for their supper that night; but

Hlaka lit many fires, moving from one as soon as there came a flash from a gun below, and lighting another a little way off, and going on again to another as soon as another shell came. But by the time he had eight or nine fires he left them burning, and moved with all his rifles and stores to another part of the Mountain.

They went along the slope to the east, and further up, to where the wild sheep lived, above any vegetation except small and scattered trees. There they found more caves and spent some hours going backwards and forwards, bringing their rifles to them, and carrying up goatskins full of water, for they were above the springs. The caves were wider and longer than the ones they had known, as though the wind and the frost had worked with more freedom at that height; but they were no deeper, for the layer of softer rock that the wind scooped was of the same width all over the Mountain.

On the sandy floor of one of these caves Srebnitz slept for some hours, but when cold hints of dawn could be seen from the Mountain, Hlaka sent him out to watch on the rocky face that looked towards the city, for he anticipated some revenge of the Germans for their defeat. The light widened in the vast view, and dawn appeared, and Srebnitz faintly heard the sound of a few volleys far off in the town, but no other sign than these was made by the Germans.

When the sun came clear into sight others came out on to the face of the Mountain, and Srebnitz went back to a narrow ravine in which the cook had lit a fire, and reported to Hlaka that no Germans had left the city or done anything he could notice, except to carry out a few executions. Hlaka listened gravely to all Srebnitz had to say, and said nothing himself. Then he went to the little fire where the others were, and they asked him how many Germans he had seen; and, when he said None, they too seemed uneasy. Even the cook stopped in the midst of a smile, to hear him, and a thoughtful look came on his face. Srebnitz turned a questioning look to Gregor.

"You see," said Gregor, "they should attack now. We beat them badly, so they won't like us. And we shall never be so few again. So now is their chance."

"But do you want them to attack us?" asked Srebnitz.

"No," said Gregor, "but Hlaka thought they would attack at dawn and, if there is no sign of them yet, Hlaka doesn't know what they are going to do. He nearly always knows what they are going to do. We can't fight fifteen to five thousand if he doesn't know everything."

"How does he know?" asked Srebnitz.

"I don't know that," said Gregor. "He fought them years ago, and he knows the Germans."

"Yes, he knows them," said the cook.

"It makes it difficult for us," said Gregor, "when we don't know what the Germans are going to do. And Hlaka is troubled."

"They bombed the Mountain yesterday," said Srebnitz.

"Yes," said Gregor. "Hlaka thought they would, and thought that might be all. But it isn't."

"How do you know?" asked Srebnitz.

"Hlaka says so," said Gregor.

"But why?" asked Srebnitz.

"He knows," Gregor said. "For one thing they didn't boast last night on the wireless that they had killed us all. If they had been at all content with their bombing, they would have done that. So they are going to do something more, and Hlaka won't be easy till he finds out. I have never known him not to be able to say what the Germans are going to do."

"He must be a wonderful man," said Srebnitz.

"He is," said Gregor. "And they are very methodical. You soon get to know their ways."

Nobody else said much, for they were all puzzled, and were all uneasy because Hlaka was unsure. And Srebnitz ate his breakfast in silence. Then they all walked out of the little ravine on to the southern slope and gazed over rocks at the city, but could see no sign of movement of any Germans coming towards the Mountain.

Much of that day they spent in putting their rifles and stores away in their new hiding-places. But Hlaka stood on the Mountain behind a rock nearly as tall as himself, and gazed towards the city for hours. At dinner all seemed shadowed by Hlaka's uneasiness, and there was little talk and no song. And Hlaka sat silent among them, like a dumb prophet. He had made no pretence to be a prophet, but there on the Mountain with his little band of men knowledge of what his mighty enemy was likely to do was so necessary that a kind of intuition was called up in him by the sore

need of The Land. When dinner was over he strode away to
the rocky slope once more and gazed again at the city, and
still in vain. Not even an aeroplane came over. Srebnitz
he sent away along the tops of the Mountain to shoot one or
two wild sheep, for their supply of meat was low. For the
rest of that day he searched the caves in which they hid, and
peered over ridges into high steep valleys in which they
sometimes fed, and often saw their tracks, but never came up
with them. Then the sun set in a splendour of scarlet clouds;
and darkness, following upon sunset closer than it does in
more northern latitudes, began to fall all round him.

Srebnitz turned homeward to the caves that were his only
home now and, as he turned, heard a pebble fall on the mountain. He turned back again and went to look over a ridge
not many paces away, and there he saw a flock of fifty wild
sheep moving behind a great-horned leader, going down the
northern slope of the Mountain. He put up his rifle, but
could not properly see the sight. He might have wounded
one, had he fired many shots, but he neither wished to wound
one of these fine animals, nor saw any use in doing so, and
did not dare to waste cartridges. For a long time he saw the
brown patch that they made on the mountain, always moving
downwards, until he was sure they were heading for the
green plain to the north, a thing he had not expected wild
sheep to do till the last man was dead.

Darkness fell long before he came to the caves, and he
moved slowly in the night over those rocks, under the light
of the moon, till he was guided home by the glow of a small

fire that Hlaka's men had lit in the ravine to help him, where its light was hidden from the town.

There he found Hlaka and all his men by the fire, and told what he had seen, not expecting to be believed.

But Hlaka said: "Yes, they do that. They know when war is coming to the Mountain. They did it last time, and I have heard they have often done it before, and the eldest leads them and they go to other mountains away to the north. They say they will do a hundred miles in a night. I don't know how they know the way, or how they know what war is. But there are a great many things I don't know."

He was silent awhile and no one spoke. If there were many things that Hlaka did not know, there was little for any other of them to say. And he repeated "Many things," and was silent again. Silent and grave. Then he lifted his head and smiled, and said: "Indeed I only know one thing: that we will free The Land."

Suddenly he was silent, and listening, motionless as a rock. And after a while a step was heard on the mountain by other men, and a dark shape appeared, till the firelight fell on it, and a man walked up to them and said: "I have come to join Hlaka."

And many more men came that night to the Mountain, from which the wild sheep had gone away on their great journey. One by one they came, or in twos and threes, all through the night; and the fire was kept glowing softly to guide them in. And before dawn came there were exactly forty-nine, the number that Hlaka had mentioned to the titular Bishop of Ilion.

But while these men were slipping quietly into the camp of Hlaka, and before many of them had yet arrived, Srebnitz had gone again to watch on the mountain, in the hope of gaining some hint of the mystery that puzzled Hlaka, and perhaps discovering what the Germans meant to do, attempting to avenge their defeat. All was dark and silent; even the moon was clouded; and in the darkness Hlaka had not yet divined anything.

And suddenly the clue came to Srebnitz out of the night. Far away down by the pine-wood, through which he had come from the town on the night when he got his rifle, he saw a light flashing. He watched the rapid flashes and tried to remember them, and did remember the first few: they went short short short, long long long, short short short, short short short, long long long, short; and after that Srebnitz could remember no more, nor keep pace with the rest. There were not many more letters, and then the light stopped. He did not know the Morse code, and knew that it was as important in the life he was leading now, as the art of Caxton himself in a calmer age. Sadly he knew that he must confess his ignorance to Hlaka. But he had a piece of pencil in his pocket and an old envelope, which he tore open, for he could not see on which side the writing was: then he dotted down the dots and dashes as far as he remembered them, and waited, gazing down towards the pine-wood with the pencil in his hand, to see if the signal would come again. And it came when he was quite ready, just as though the signaller had waited for this; the same shorts and longs as before, and then went on with two longs. His memory had failed him just in the middle of a letter, where the regular arrangement of shorts and longs had changed: that letter was short long long, and was followed by four shorts, and then by two shorts, and then by a short and a long. He waited yet, and the message was repeated a third time. And he checked it and found that he had it right, and took it back to Hlaka. He went up to Hlaka by the fire and confessed: he said, "I cannot read Morse."

Hlaka looked at him and said nothing. Then he showed Hlaka the actual message in dots and dashes, that he had written down. And Hlaka took it and read it. Nothing in his expression changed.

"Yes," he said. "I know now what they will do."

XII

WHEN Hlaka had spoken he sat quite silent awhile, gazing into the fire. But when it seemed that his plans were made, he lifted his head and spoke quickly. "We must march," he said. "They are attacking women."

Then he sent three men to reply to the signal from different points; merely four dots from electric torches, signalling the letter H. Then he told his men where they must go, for Hlaka's men did not march in fours or in threes, but moved more like hunting dogs, not going one behind the other, but each one knowing where the others are: to the pine-wood first, he said; and then to a house which he described at the near end of the town; and, as he described it, Srebnitz began to see that it was the house of the two old ladies. "I know that house," he exclaimed.

"Then you will be the scout," said Hlaka. "Go to the pine-wood and find who signalled. If you cannot find anyone, go on to the house. But, before you go into the town, come back and leave your rifle with Gregor, who will wait outside the wood."

The cook was to stay by the little fire that was hidden in the ravine and receive the rest of the men that were coming in to join Hlaka, while several of these men themselves were to go to different points on the Mountain to guide the rest. If Hlaka was not back by dawn the cook was to get Srebnitz's air-gun and test all the newcomers, and train them as well as he could.

Srebnitz and Gregor started off together, and saw no more of the others nor even heard them; but Gregor told him that they were close, though he could not see or hear them either. Sometimes a pebble rolled away, like the one the wild sheep had dislodged, but there was no other sound, so the whole force of Hlaka marched in dead silence. Their progress was slow over the rocks in the dark, and neither Srebnitz nor Gregor spoke, except for an occasional word in a low voice from Gregor to guide Srebnitz past some obstacle. At last they came to the road, where it ended below their old camping-ground. And, now that they could walk without difficulty, Gregor and Srebnitz began to talk in low voices.

"So you know the house," said Gregor.

"Yes," said Srebnitz. "What is happening there?"

"I think the Germans are attacking it," said Gregor.

"But two old ladies live there," Srebnitz said. "They are most inoffensive and harmless. And there is a girl there."

"They are just the people the Germans would attack," Gregor answered. "They have men called psychologists, who work out what people like us feel. Their plan is to hurt us by hurting others; and the more inoffensive the people they hurt, the more they think it will hurt us."

"What will they do to them?" asked Srebnitz.

"I don't know," said Gregor. "If you find no one in the wood, you must go to the house and find out, and come back and tell me, and then we will all go."

"What was the message?" asked Srebnitz.

"It was an S.O.S.," said Gregor.

For a while they walked in silence, while all manner of dark fears passed through Srebnitz's mind. He could not believe that they would hurt Sophia, or rather he would not believe it; but he remembered how he had not thought they could kill his father and mother, and his fears overwhelmed his struggle to believe that Sophia was safe. He asked Gregor a few anxious and idle questions, whose answers could not be known. Then they went on in silence.

Srebnitz hurried, but Gregor checked him, for they would have got too far ahead of the rest. It was the road that Srebnitz had taken when he had come from the town, the only road up the Mountain, but it looked all different at night.

The moon was behind the Mountain and they had no light now but stars, and the faint gleam of the road. Then they came to that part of the road that Srebnitz had walked by night; and, though he could recognize no feature of it in the darkness, the Mountain seemed to look at him with the same expression with which it had looked at him when he was coming away from the pine-wood; for mountains like people alter their attitude to us as we alter ours to them, and by the appearance of the line of crags against the sky Srebnitz knew his whereabouts.

Again the idle questions from Srebnitz as to what the Germans would do to the women in that house. But he, like Gregor, had heard the volleys at dawn, and was as well informed in such matters as the man from whom he so wistfully sought information.

Then the dark shape of the pine-wood came into sight, and Gregor repeated to Srebnitz his instructions, which were to search the wood for whoever had sent the message, and, if finding no one, to go on to the house in which the two old ladies lived, and to find out what was wrong, and come back and tell Gregor. Gregor would wait on the road to take Srebnitz's rifle from him, if he should have to go on to the town. He had not reminded Srebnitz to bring his knife, any more than clerks in London are reminded to bring their fountain-pens; for to carry a knife is a habit amongst that people.

Then Srebnitz went alone into the wood. He left the

road, in case there were Germans in the wood, for he would have shown up against the grey road, whereas everyone in the wood was in equal darkness. From tree to tree he went slowly right through the wood on the left-hand side of the road, then moved further still to his left and came quietly back. Then he went towards the road, intending to cross it and to explore the wood on the other side. Just as he came to the point from which he had started, he heard the sound of a dry twig crack behind him. He spun round with his rifle ready, and heard a quiet voice ask him, as though seeking information. "You are not going to shoot? Are you?"

It was Sophia. And once again Srebnitz had the feeling, so out of place in the sinister gloom of that wood, that Sophia might be laughing at him.

"Sophia!" exclaimed Srebnitz.

"Yes," said Sophia.

"Did you send that message?" he asked.

"Yes," she replied.

"What was it?" said Srebnitz.

"S.O.S., Sophia," she answered.

So that was what it was.

"What is the matter?" he asked.

"The Germans are interrogating my aunts," she said.

"Asking them questions?" said Srebnitz.

"Interrogating them," repeated Sophia.

There was somehow some difference; and from Sophia's tone of voice Srebnitz got the idea that the difference was an ominous one.

"Are they still there?" asked Srebnitz.

"They were there not long ago," said Sophia. "I went back to watch after sending the message, and have only just come here to meet you."

"How did you know I should see your message at once?" he asked.

"I didn't send it to you," she said.

"Not to me?" he said.

"No," said Sophia.

"To whom then?" he asked.

"To Hlaka," she said.

"Hlaka!" he exclaimed.

"Yes," she said. "Did you think I was signalling to you?"

"No," said Srebnitz. "But does Hlaka know your name?"

"Yes," she said. "Does that surprise you?"

"No," he said. "And do you know Hlaka?"

"I know him very well," she said.

"Of course a great many people do," said Srebnitz.

"Of course," said Sophia.

He was not satisfied, but there was no time for more talk.

"How many Germans are there in your aunts' house?" he asked her.

"Five," she said. "One at the front door, none at the back, and two officers inside the house with a corporal and private."

"What rooms are they in?" he asked.

"The officers are in the room you know," she said, "and the other two are just outside in the passage."

"Have they been there ever since you sent the message?" asked Srebnitz.

"Yes," said Sophia, "two of them pouring out questions all the time. They won't stop until my aunts have said something they want them to say. And they'll never do that."

"And then?" said Srebnitz.

"You must come quickly," said Sophia.

To march through the streets with rifles seemed impossible, and how to deal, without them, with five armed men close together Srebnitz could not see.

"I must tell Hlaka," he said.

"Is he here?" asked Sophia.

"Yes," said Srebnitz, "quite close."

Sophia's face lit up, but the light that romantic fancies light in the face of a lad went out of Srebnitz's face at the same moment, as a field in April goes dim and greeny-grey, while the green of another field close to it turns almost to gold.

"Will you still be here?" asked Srebnitz.

"Yes," said Sophia, "if you are not gone too long."

Then Srebnitz went back to Gregor, and told him what he had heard, and said they must find Hlaka.

"Don't speak so loud," said a voice near to him. And it was Hlaka. Srebnitz repeated to him his information. And Hlaka said, "We must go to the house." Then he uttered one of the many cries that an owl makes at night, and very soon his men were all round him.

"We must go into the town," he said. "We will leave our rifles at the far end of the wood, with Mihail to look after them. There are only four men in the house and one outside. I will deal with the first three."

One by one he gave brief instructions to his men in a low voice, then led the way down the road to the edge of the wood. There he stopped his men with one sign of his hand, and walked a little way into the wood with Sophia. Srebnitz could not hear what they said. Then they all went through the wood in their usual marching order, that is to say not far away from each other, but each man taking his own line and slipping from tree to tree, like a tree's shadow going quietly through the night to visit its neighbour. At the far end of the wood they left their rifles with that one of Hlaka's men who was called Mihail, and Sophia remained with him. With Mihail also they all left their boots.

Then they hurried on down the road to the town. No street-lamps were burning there, but a rare light twinkled here and there from a window. For the Germans knew that the Allies would not bomb this city. As they came to the edge of the town, Hlaka halted them and told Srebnitz to keep close to him and to get into the garden of the old ladies' house as far as he could without being seen; and Iskander he told to come also, and to shoot either through the window or in the house itself when the door should be opened, as opportunity offered. "For I am afraid it must come to shooting," said Hlaka. "And we must go away very fast with the old ladies as soon as that has happened."

"But we have no rifles," said Srebnitz to Iskander.

"We shall pick one up in the garden," Iskander said.

While Hlaka was speaking to Srebnitz in a low voice, standing close, Srebnitz noticed for the first time that he now wore very ragged clothes and carried a long stick.

Then Hlaka's army marched on, as it always marched, not like soldiers, but shadows, separate shadows that, with their bare feet on the pavement, moved now like worthy recruits for a regiment of the guards of the King of Shadows. Dark, without any sound whatever, they moved through the dark streets, shadow by shadow, like the shadows of the iron clamps of a lantern following one another as the lantern is twirled in a hand. Unseen they went down the street that led into the town, unseen they passed the two larger intersecting streets and reached the lane that Srebnitz knew, the lane whose romance seemed once to belong to Srebnitz, but nothing seemed to belong to anyone now except to the grim Hlaka. Under the fruit-trees they went, and came to the gate in the garden through which Sophia had once brought Srebnitz, and passed it and, turning up a narrow street to their right, soon came to the street on which looked, over a little garden, the front windows and door of the house they sought. They turned again to their right, Hlaka leading; then he made a swift sign with his hand to caution Iskander and Srebnitz, and the house of the old ladies came in sight.

The great stature of Hlaka fell forward with the suddenness of an avalanche in spring on the Mountain, and the bulk of his chest seemed to decrease, and with drooping head and stooped figure he went forward, tapping as he went with his stick. At once was heard the rattle of a rifle being brought down from the slope.

"Halt!" shouted the sentry from the doorstep of the old ladies' house.

"I am blind," came the voice of Hlaka.

"What are you doing here?" shouted the sentry.

"I have lost my way," said Hlaka. "Show me my way home."

And he turned in by the little gateway and hobbled up the path, with a look of decrepitude and yet with speed, as a wounded rat might move.

"This is not your way," shouted the sentry.

"Show me my way," whined Hlaka.

"What are you doing out at night?" said the sentry, pointing his bayonet at him. But still Hlaka hobbled on.

"Night is my day," he said, "as it is to all whose day is night."

That puzzled the sentry, and for a moment he tried to make sense of it; and, while his wits were so occupied, Hlaka stabbed him. He signed then to Srebnitz, who ran up and received the rifle from Hlaka. Hlaka had been speaking German and continued to speak it, speaking about a permit to be out after curfew and profusely thanking the sentry, who lay quite dead. Meanwhile he knocked at the door, three rather timid knocks. The door was opened.

"A message for the captain," said Hlaka. "I am sent because I am blind, and night is no darker to me than day."

And he began to fumble for the message among his rags.

Srebnitz saw two men inside the door, and Hlaka swaying slightly as he fumbled, and moving his position as he swayed. The curtain had been drawn partly back from the window of the room in which the old ladies sat and the blind had been raised, perhaps so that the sentry could see into the room. But those in the bright light could not see the sentry.

In a flash that left a picture long in his memory Srebnitz saw the whole room, the mantelpiece with two china candlesticks on it with little china figures holding the candles, two humming-birds each in a domed glass case, and a small clock in the middle; a velvet overmantel and small pictures in velvet frames, two comfortable armchairs dressed in chintzes with a design of small roses, and the old ladies in the chairs still knitting, and two ferocious Prussian officers talking rapidly one after the other.

This Srebnitz saw in a flash, before his eyes turned back to Hlaka. Hlaka seemed to be shifting his position so as to get close in front of the first man, but the other man was peering round his shoulder and evidently looking for the sentry. Suddenly he raised his rifle. At this moment the first man fell in a heap on the floor with no more sound than a gasp, and Hlaka leapt on the man behind him. Iskander rushed past Srebnitz into the doorway; and Srebnitz saw that he would have a clearer view through the window, as the two officers went to the sitting-room door to see what was wrong in the passage, and drew their pistols as they went. One officer actually did reach the passage, but at that mo-

ment Srebnitz broke the window-pane with his bayonet, and
the second officer turned and raised his pistol, and Srebnitz
fired first. That was the only shot fired, for Iskander ran
right into the other officer like a footballer, and killed him
with his knife before he had time to fire. Only one shot was
better than Hlaka had hoped; yet there is no mistaking a
shot at night in a town, so there was little time to spare.

Iskander signed to Srebnitz to come in quickly, and
dragged the sentry in and shut the door and took one of the
rifles, while Hlaka picked up another.

"Dear me," said Isabella.

Angelica smiled and said nothing.

"Now to the Mountain," said Hlaka.

XIII

HLAKA seized a hand of Isabella and hurried her through the
kitchen as though he knew the way. With a wave of his head
and a look he signed to Iskander to do the same with Angelica.

"I must bring a few things," said Isabella.

"There is no time," said Hlaka.

"We had everything ready, in case it happened," said
Isabella. "We have all we want in two sacks."

"Where are they?" asked Hlaka, as they came to the back
door.

"Beside our beds," said Isabella. "We can get them in a minute."

"You should have kept them downstairs," said Hlaka. "There's not a minute to spare."

"We should very much like them," said Angelica.

"Get them," said Hlaka to Srebnitz. "Give me your rifle."

"Two satin bags," said Angelica, "each on a chair by our beds."

Hlaka slung Srebnitz's bayoneted rifle over his shoulder. His own was in his left hand. With his right hand he seized Isabella's left hand again and hurried her through the garden. He relied on Srebnitz's young speed to overtake them, but his own speed was now that of Isabella and of Angelica: the seconds he gained with them over delay, the yards he could run with them, before the shot woke the town, were all that he now thought of.

Srebnitz ran upstairs to the two bedrooms, and found the satin sacks just where Isabella had said. It's cold on the Mountain, he thought. There was a large cupboard in each room, and Srebnitz looked in both and brought the two thickest coats. All the neat dresses hanging there seemed to wear a forlorn look, a look not easily described to any who have not seen a doomed house, known at once to those who have. As Srebnitz gazed at them he heard steps in the street. From one of the beds he seized two blankets and ran downstairs. Then a thought came to him that should have come before: a dead man lay in the sitting-room, and the curtains were drawn back. He ran, and the steps came nearer. There was no time to draw the curtains, or time to blow out six candles, three on each of the little china candelabras, held by bright Dresden figures. So he threw both to the floor. As they fell he saw the pistol of the German officer that he had shot, lying beside him.

The steps came nearer, two men, not running, but evidently coming to investigate, for they were walking fast. Would they guess which house it was in which the shot had been fired? Srebnitz hoped not. For though he had learned Hlaka's way of feeling the master of these men, and knew he could easily defend himself, yet he knew that more shooting, and from the same house, was certain to bring so many Germans that Hlaka's whole force might be endangered. One shot was different; it might be accidental. And yet the Germans scarcely seemed to think so, for now he heard more feet marching, a patrol of several men. As Srebnitz picked up the pistol the two men passed the door. There must be another pistol in the passage. So he got that too, and put them both in his pockets. They might be useful on the Mountain, thought Srebnitz; but the thought led to the question of ammunition. He searched both bodies in the dark, and found two small pouches holding twenty more cartridges each. As he took the cartridges from the officer in the sitting-room, the patrol came close. Though much encumbered with coats and blankets over his shoulder, and the two satin bags, he had a hand to spare, with which to snatch a fresh ham as he ran through the kitchen. The back-door was open. He ran through and shut it, but did not stop to lock it, for the chief danger seemed to him to be from the streets ahead, and that increased every second.

All seemed quiet at the back, as he ran through the dark garden, and all seemed quiet in the lane; but soon a hand clutched his arm as he ran: it was Gregor, who had waited for him, and took from him the two satin bags, and then ran on beside him. "I've a pistol for you," said Srebnitz.

"Put it in my pocket," said Gregor, with a satin bag in each hand.

Srebnitz did so as they ran.

Before they came to the end of the dark lane they saw the shapes of the others. They were all together now. And two men ran one on each side of Angelica and holding her hands, and two more helped Isabella. Hlaka was glancing anxiously at the old ladies, almost watching each breath, for upon their pace depended everything. When one glimmering window showed that they came near streets again he made two of his men carry them, still running, so as to rest them.

They came to the street, and all was quiet. There they spread out in their old way, going on their bare feet like separate shadows. There they put the two old ladies down, but their shoes made a sound on the pavement as they walked. So two men carried them again. Still all was quiet in the street.

Now they approached the wide street that they had to cross, and no sound came from that either. Then a distant lorry was heard, down the street to their left. But it stopped, and all was silent again. They neared the wide street now, and hopes were high.

Suddenly there flashed before them, only a few yards away, the great beam of a searchlight right down the midst of the street that they had to cross. Hlaka halted his men as they came level with him, and waited. But the searchlight did not move or even flicker, and remained a great barrier across their way. At the same time they heard a patrol marching up the middle of the road.

Still as the shadows of trees stood Hlaka's men. The patrol marched past the end of the street they were in, eight of them, every figure clear in the searchlight within twelve yards of Hlaka, and marched on up the wide street. Hlaka raised his hand to keep his men where they were and slipped on into the wide street, silently as a night-bird leaving its branch. At the corner of the street he beckoned, and all his men came up to him. The pavement was in darkness, and the whole road was lit. The searchlight that lit it was a hundred yards away on a lorry. The lorry was facing away from him, illuminating the street beyond with its own two lamps. Every stone in the road shone clear as jewellery, but nearer the lorry there was darkness between the beam and the road. To this darkness Hlaka pointed, and led his men fifty yards nearer the lorry, two of them still carrying the old ladies. Fifty yards from the lorry he stopped them, where the beam was a foot and a half from the ground.

Then he crawled into the road, and lay under the beam

and signed to them all to do the same. He lifted a hand and
held it near to the beam, and made them all pass under
his hand. More steps were heard marching up from the
town, but they were a long way off and the sound went far
in the night. Hlaka's men had only a few yards to crawl,
while the others marched two hundred. They all crawled
quickly under Hlaka's hand, even the two old ladies. Moths
showed vividly in the beam, with all their colours gleaming,
while Hlaka's men went unseen; and the last of them passed
under the beam by the time the patrol had marched up to
the lorry. The far pavement was dark like the other, and
still the beam never moved.

They hurried along the pavement and came to the crossing, and turned to their left, and the barrier of light was
behind them. They knew that the patrol that was behind
them would turn either to left or right when it came to the
cross-roads, because there was another patrol so close in
front of it; and Hlaka, with the knowledge he had of such
things, knew it would turn to the left. Yet they were marching at the usual pace, while Hlaka's men were running.

If they met no obstacle, they need not fear the patrol.
But, if anything stopped them in front, they might be caught
in a trap.

They crossed the next street safely.

Hlaka had made the old ladies go amongst the first under
the beam, so as to give the slowest all the start he could, and
the slowest were bound to be the men that carried Isabella
and Angelica, even though Hlaka relieved them before they
were tired.

Another crossing was passed in safety, the last, and once more hopes were high. Again came danger ahead of them. They had gained much on the patrol that was marching behind them; but now Hlaka saw two lights swinging across the road ahead, which were electric torches carried by two men who were coming down the road towards his men. He noted quickly their method and the rhythmic swing of their lights; then he gave his rifle and bayonet to Srebnitz, because he was the youngest and able to move quicker than Hlaka could, and gave quick orders to him and Iskunder, and to another man who had a rifle and bayonet. They were to lie down in the road in front of the two men, who were only swinging their light about fifteen yards ahead of them: they must wait until they were seen, and then run at the men and bayonet them. Meanwhile Hlaka kept onward, and did not halt his little force until the two men were close. Thus the patrol behind gained barely thirty yards on them.

The three young men that were to run at the two were out in front of the rest. Soon they saw the two men coming, but the two did not see them, because their eyes, relying on artificial light, could see little that was not lighted by their torches. They were two soldiers, with rifles slung, and carrying electric torches in their right hands. The lights went methodically across the road to and fro, never more than fifteen yards in front of them.

Hlaka had ordered that there must be no firing by his men, and none allowed by the Germans. To carry out the last part of the order Srebnitz knew would be impossible without the best start that a runner could make. He watched the light of the torches meeting about the middle of the road, and swinging regularly to left and right as the two men came on. Meanwhile he heard the patrol coming nearer, behind him. And now the two men were within fifteen yards, and the lights were swinging into the middle of the road. They met only a few inches in front of the three men that were waiting, and swung out again to the pavements.

Srebnitz got up and ran forward, and got five yards before a light came back and caught him. The other two got up immediately after, and raced forward with Srebnitz. Had the Germans not had torches in their hands, there would have perhaps been time. They threw the torches down and unslung their rifles, and got them up to their shoulders; but time, that is so great an ingredient of war, allowed them no more than that. Three bayonets struck the two Germans. One of them shouted.

And Hlaka's men ran on, all but two whom he told to get the two rifles, and the ammunition in the belts if they could get it before the patrol saw them.

But the patrol had heard the shout and was now coming on at a run.

So they left the ammunition, taking only the loaded rifles; for, if they had been seen and fired at, they feared that the sound of the firing would wake the town too wide. They ran on before they were seen, gaining easily on the patrol, which sounded to be from eight to a dozen men, and soon overtook the rest; but these were not gaining; so Hlaka told the men that were carrying the two ladies to put them down and to run beside them again holding their hands. He risked the sound of their feet being heard now, for the patrol must know that they were before it in any case, as the two men in the road had just been killed, and the men who did it had not gone past the patrol, and the road led only one other way, so that the men behind must know they were off to the Mountain.

Speed was the important thing now. Isabella and Angelica ran lightly, and were not heard by the patrol, above the sound of the Germans' own boots. Hlaka's party were once more gaining. They had only another hundred and fifty yards to go, and they would be out of the town in wild land that sloped up to the Mountain. There they would feel safe, like wild things in their coverts.

But at this moment Hlaka heard, and all of them, the sound of the engines of a lorry behind them. It was the lorry that had illuminated the street they had crossed: it was not the smooth roar of an engine running, but the troubled uneasy muttering of an engine being turned round. For the engine was luckily facing the wrong way. It had only a hundred yards to get to the cross-roads; but it was not yet turned round. Hlaka's men must have run fifty yards by the time the lorry was turned; then it moved forward a few yards no faster than they were going, gained speed and rushed to the crossing. There, instead of turning to the left and pursuing them, it turned to the right, in order to illuminate the street in which they ran before the patrol. They saw the flash of the beam swing right across the street, and were still twenty yards from the end. Then they heard the grating of gears as the engines were reversed, and the lorry came up the street behind them, and its wandering beam began to peer down the street to look for them.

Once it nearly caught them, but just fell short where the road heaved over a culvert, and sent a great shadow rushing at them. Then it lit up the patrol, and they saw it marching in threes.

And at that moment Hlaka and the two ladies came to the last houses. The road, as it left the town, forsook its orderly straightness immediately and took a turn to its right. And round the last house on the right Hlaka's men ran into darkness. Through the first gap in the hedge on the right they all ran, and the hedge on the left was illuminated by the weird beam of the searchlight before the last one was through. There they lay down in a line behind the hedge.

Five of Hlaka's men now had rifles, and two had pistols, and all had knives; but he did not wish to fight while the two ladies were with him, if a fight could be avoided. Though only twenty yards from the edge of the town, his men felt a new confidence, that seemed to flow into their hearts down the dark slope of the Mountain; while the patrol that came out from the city with the searchlight close behind them, as they saw the open land and the night and the Mountain before them, felt that they crossed the frontier of an unfamiliar country.

The patrol did not leave the road to search for Hlaka's men in the wide night, but marched on down it for half a

mile and then returned to the town; while the men on the
lorry turned the searchlight round, and then the lorry, and
drove it a long way up the road, where it looked like a great
comet that had come to visit the Mountain.

As soon as the patrol was a hundred and fifty yards past
them, Hlaka marched his men on down the road behind
them; and, when it turned, he led his men back again to the
dark of the untamed land. Then the lorry turned back. The
beam was sweeping on each side of the road as it came towards the town, and there was scarcely any cover where
Hlaka's men now lay, except the darkness of night. Some
thought of attacking the lorry seemed to come to Hlaka's
men, as some of them rose to their hands and knees and
looked at him. But the patrol was too close behind for that,
and he went forward alone. Hlaka was lost to sight of his
men at once, and the lorry came nearer with its great searching beam, till the huge shadows leaping up from it were
close to the mountaineers. And then they heard one shot,
and the light went out. The shot had come from the far side
of the road from the one on which Hlaka had left his men,
and in that direction men from the lorry pursued him, and
some of the patrol went to help them, while the rest stood still
and watched. And they pursued until they all perceived the
vanity of trying to overtake Hlaka on the slope of the Mountain by night.

XIV

OVER the open country Hlaka's men, with Isabella and Angelica, moved towards the pine-wood. But when the lorry, with its blinded searchlight, returned to the town, and there was no more sound of marching, they went back to the road, where walking was easier for the two ladies. Before long they came to the pine-wood. Srebnitz peered into the wood, and did not at first see Mihail; he stood too still, with dark clothes, in the darkness.

Then he saw a patch of dress, less dim than the wood, and Sophia was coming towards him. For whom did she look? But her first question was, "Where is Hlaka?"

"He'll be here soon," said Srebnitz, and went to the others to pick up the rifles they had left in the wood, and to divide the things to be carried besides.

All this they did hastily, for their great home towered above them, and it was late, and the feeling for home that all men have at such an hour, and after a hard day, was coming upon them. The city was still not far, with its pavements, its closed doors, its rules and its regulations, now intensified by men who loved regulations and were against all that is free. And they yearned for the Mountain, which gave them freedom with welcoming hands and would one day free The Land. So each of them picked up his rifle, and put on his boots, and five of them slung a new rifle over their shoulders, and all took the mountain road. And before they had trodden it long, Hlaka was marching among them.

As the slope of the Mountain began to heave against them, the men might have felt fatigue after their long night; but, cheered by the dark shape of their rocky home, they climbed with a new vigour, and all the cares that trouble men in cities were soon far below them.

To Isabella and Angelica, who often sitting in their armchairs with calm and unmoved faces, while Sophia went to and fro, were reading tales of romantic adventure, this night on the Mountain, and even the bloodshed in their house, were as though steps had been taken, which perhaps had once not seemed likely, but which were nevertheless but a little way from the land of their dreams to tho land of this strange reality. And so when the man who had been questioning them dropped dead in their sitting-room, the contrast between the corpse and their velvet overmantel was not so much the scene that stamped itself on their memory, as the sight of the dream come true.

To Sophia all the world was full of romance: it was even in her aunts' house in the town, more in the garden, more still in the lane under the fruit-trees, and most of all somewhere between the twilight on the Mountain and the stars.

So, among armed men on the Mountain, the aunts were in scenes they had read of, and Sophia was walking where her dreams had been, so that to neither did the adventure seem unfamiliar.

Sophia was walking with Hlaka, and Srebnitz walked a little apart in silence. If it was jealousy that he felt, it might seem out of place where any man of Hlaka's age was the cause; and Sophia was barely seventeen. But there was an energy about Hlaka that defied age, as he had defied the Germans with his army of fifteen men, and was even now defying all Germany, confident that her armies would be beaten back to her borders. So Srebnitz walked alone. And after a while Sophia came up to him. He heard her voice beside him before he heard her step.

"Did you get a good rifle?" she asked.

"I don't know," he said.

For a little while there was silence.

And then Sophia said, "It was kind of you to get my aunts' things."

Suddenly it seemed to Srebnitz that Sophia might not be lost to him for ever. And, as he had just thought that she was, his new thought fitted so ill with his former thought that he could not make head or tail of either of them. He realised, now, that he had answered gruffly about the rifle, and said, with some thought of making amends: "I brought a ham too. I hope I did right."

"Yes," said Sophia. "They'll burn the house now."

"They'll burn it!" exclaimed Srebnitz. "Why?"

"Because they can't burn my aunts and me," said Sophia.

"If they did that . . . !" said Srebnitz.

"What would you do?" asked Sophia.

"I would lock many of them into a house," said Srebnitz, "and burn them alive."

"That would be very unkind," said Sophia.

"Very," said Srebnitz.

And his vehement word broke the thread of some playful remark that Sophia had planned to make, and for a while both were silent, while thoughts arose in the mind of the young man that were worthy of Sophia and attuned to the solemnity of the Mountain, but would not break into words. Nor would anyone find words easy for the thoughts that were in his mind, for they looked on Sophia as somehow akin to the Mountain. She seemed to his fancy to have little to do with the house of her aunts, or with any houses, something to do with their garden, more with the lane under the lemon trees, and most of all with the Mountain. And words might trace what was eternal in Sophia and what was eternal in the Mountain, and what each had in common with the stars, but such words do not come easily, and to Srebnitz they had not yet come at all; when a golden light, too large and bright for a star, a light like a small sun, fell slowly towards the far end of the Mountain.

"How lovely!" exclaimed Sophia.

But the loveliness of the small sun was deceptive. It was a light dropped by an aeroplane, and many a man that has seen that sunny glow by night has never seen the real sun rise again. Two of Hlaka's men did not, new men who had come to the Mountain only that night and had not yet learned Hlaka's lesson to go unseen: the bomb that followed the star found them still gazing at the golden light, and scattered their broken bodies over the mountain. Sophia and Srebnitz, and all who marched with Hlaka, saw the night leap away from the flash of the bomb, where an insane daylight shone for a frantic instant; and, when night came back to the peaks, they heard it troubled for long with the wandering reverberations that roamed from the single explosion. Above the last of the mutterings the explosion made to the peaks they heard the throbbing of the engines of aeroplanes, and a flight of bombers was coming along the Mountain, dropping golden stars as they came.

Before the first bomb fell, at the sight of the first gold star, Hlaka had led the old ladies from the road and showed them where to hide amongst the heath, and a single word from him had scattered his men. Srebnitz led Sophia quickly to a patch of myrtle, and concealed her and hid himself; and the bombers above the ridge came by with their golden stars, from which long shadows leaped wildly, wakened and routed with the retreating darkness, but they did not discover any of Hlaka's men, and no more bombs were dropped. Then the batteries outside the town opened, and fired shrapnel at the place where the first bomb had dropped; but of this Hlaka took no notice, and collected his party again and went on up the road.

"Their spirits are low because we beat them," he said.

Srebnitz gazed uneasily at the shrapnel, whose intensely red burst seemed to be just where the cook, and the men who joined that night, were waiting for them at Hlaka's new headquarters. But Hlaka, trusting the Mountain to protect them, spoke slightingly of the guns, and, while the booming of guns and shells was running from crag to crag, said, "They are trying to hearten themselves. But it is better to beat drums."

Perhaps the economy that he himself practised with bullets had made him unduly critical of an ordinary display of gunfire. Presently the guns ceased, no more aeroplanes came over, and all the peaks were silent.

In the silence Srebnitz shivered; then he noticed that the shape of Sophia beside him, which he had rather imagined than seen, was now clearly visible; the shapes of the others were showing too, with hands and faces and even features, which had only been pieces of darkness a while ago, darker than the rest of the night; and Srebnitz looked upward, and it was dawn; dawn not yet visible with any colours, from where they walked along the face of the ridge (nor were all the stars gone), but the plains on the other side of the Mountain must have seen it, and night was already retreating. Cold and fading westwards it went away, and Srebnitz thought of the Germans and the day that his dreams saw. And when a clearer light came over the Mountain Sophia saw more than that light in Srebnitz's eyes, and knew that they shone from hope.

To the old camping-ground they came again, to the little arena among the circle of rocks, and slept in the caves near by for what was left of the night, while the sky over them seemed to be a space that the night had ravaged and that was not yet rescued by the advance of day. Hlaka gave a cave to Isabella and Angelica for themselves and Sophia, with apologies for the hardness of his mountain, to which he welcomed them with the diffidence of the host of some aged inn, and hoped that, with the coats and blankets that Srebnitz had brought, they would be able to sleep. "Not so well as the two Prussian officers," said Isabella.

"But well enough," said Angelica.

XV

WHEN morning had been long on the Mountain, Hlaka brought Sophia and her aunts from the cave to the little arena, in which a fire was once more burning. There Srebnitz's ham was roasted and cut with their sharp knives, and plates were handed round like those that man made use of thousands of years ago, smooth pieces of stone, such as war, rummaging among bygone things, brings sometimes from distant ages, to mix with inventions our day has made in his honour. And not far away was a stream, whose water was fresher than any that cities know. Sleep, food, water and warmth are four things whose value is acknowledged in times of peace and amongst ordered ways; but their value in these times and places is not known at its true worth, where so many other things, such as railway time-tables, bus-tickets and finance, have to be assessed at the same time. Here on the Mountain in time of war they stood out as four primal things.

When they had rested and warmed themselves they heaped bundles of heath and myrtle on to the fire, and left it, and, travelling along the other side of the ridge, made their way to their new headquarters, where they had left the cook.

Day shone on the plain to the north for miles and miles. Looking over The Land in the sunlight, and far away to the north, Srebnitz could see no sign that it was not free; and for a while he wondered; and then he realised rather slowly that, mighty though Hitler was, the curse that he had had the power to call up only availed against man, or that, where it blasted Nature, it harmed the green fields and forests little more than the industries of the days of peace harmed them, and indeed that many a scarred and pitted hillside would grow green again and be full of birds and flowers, far sooner than the fields that pavement and tarmac covered in miles of peaceful cities. But, however that were, a curse lay over The Land, which Srebnitz and every one of Hlaka's men were resolved and sworn to lift.

They came slowly, at the pace of Isabella and Angelica, over difficult ground, to the camp that they had left the night before, further along the range and higher up the Mountain. There all the men that had come in the night were gathered; or, rather, partially scattered, each near the rocks or cave that should give him cover as soon as an aeroplane might be seen or heard. And there the cook told Hlaka of the loss of the two men.

Hlaka remained silent: his one care was for The Land; his one thought, liberty. If he had any sympathies to spare from that care, they seemed not to be for men whom he knew must have showed themselves, and who were therefore, in Hlaka's opinion, not the kind of men who would be able to free The Land.

Then he went away to a cave to be alone with his thoughts, thoughts that to him were what music is to musicians, or research to scientists, and even more what prophecy is to prophets, thoughts that were solely concerned with what the Germans would do. That they were methodical by nature he knew, and that would tend to make them do what they had done before, as they often did; but he knew that industry had made them clever, up to the limits of which their minds were capable, so he knew they would not repeat an action that had been a failure. Therefore, Germans though they were, they would do something new.

With a strange and invisible chase the thoughts of Hlaka up there on the Mountain tried to follow the thoughts of a German general, planning down in the city. Whether or not he hunted his quarry down was never to be known, though none of his men doubted that Hlaka knew.

But before the sun that day had left the morning, to slant towards evening and the end of the Mountain, they saw a solitary figure very far off, coming up the mountain-road.

All through the afternoon they watched him, an unarmed man in civilian clothes, till he came to the end of the road, and from there was guided by one of Hlaka's men up to his camp; and he was to have much to do with Hlaka's plans. He was a barber in a small way of business in the town. Few knew him, but all greeted him as a new comrade, and he heartily greeted them. The cook brought out a bottle of one of their sweet wines, unknown even by name, in England, and he drank to The Land and to Victory.

The cook had been busy all that morning till Hlaka came, teaching the new men how to shoot at short ranges with Srebnitz's air-gun and not to shoot at all until they were hidden, and not to make metallic noises, such as are made by a rifle touching a rock, and not to wait and try for the perfect shot that would hit a button at a hundred yards, but to take the shot that was good enough when the chance occurred; and all the things that he was able to teach clearly to men in a single morning. But, when Hlaka came, he took the air-gun away and said that he would use it himself, and that the men should practise with rifles, and that any man that he could see at a hundred yards he would shoot with the air-gun. Then he made men bring a great number of blankets to one of the caves, and had it upholstered with curtains and a carpet for Sophia and her aunts. And, while he was attending to this, some of the men brought the barber to him, for he had been telling them the Germans' plans, and they brought him for Hlaka to hear them.

Hlaka sent them all away but the barber, for he did not

discuss his plans with any of them. And when they were gone he asked what the Germans intended to do. And the barber said that he had heard from a German sergeant that they were not going to attack the Mountain with any more men, but would only fire occasional shells, because they had lost too many men on the Mountain already. And the barber, who had a drinking-horn still in his hand with some of the sweet wine left in it, drank again to victory, standing before Hlaka sitting on a rock.

"Did he tell you I had a rifle for you?" asked Hlaka, jerking his head sideways towards the city.

"Yes," said the barber.

"Who?" said Hlaka.

The barber paused for an instant, and then gave some name that was not the name of the titular Bishop of Ilion.

Then Hlaka knew that he was a spy.

Hlaka nodded his head and shrugged his right shoulder.

"It is pleasant to see the sun," said Hlaka, lifting his head a little towards it, but not taking his eyes off the barber.

"It is indeed," said the man.

"Tell me what your masters are going to do," said Hlaka. "And if every word you say is the truth, you shall see the sun again."

The shrug of his right shoulder had loosened his rifle, which was over his shoulder on a strap, and brought it forward: Hlaka now held it in both hands.

"I—I . . ." said the barber.

"One word that is not the truth," said Hlaka, "and it will be the last."

The barber looked intently at him and then said: "I will tell you everything."

"Then you shall live," said Hlaka with a smile.

"I am a poor man, and they tempted me," said the barber. And he waited for some remark from Hlaka. But Hlaka said nothing.

And the barber went on: "They compelled me to come to the Mountain and to find out the number of your men."

"I have sixty-one," said Hlaka.

Somehow this sudden piece of truth disconcerted the spy. He had not yet counted the men, but he saw from Hlaka's face that it was the truth.

"And to find out your plans," continued the barber.

"I will tell you my plans," said Hlaka, "when I know theirs."

And he looked up at the sun, though one eye still watched the barber. And that was the eye that really watched, for the glance towards the sun was only a gesture. Once more the barber looked at Hlaka intently, and sighed. Then he did what he had not done much for many years, and told the truth. "They will completely surround the Mountain with all their men," he said.

"That is right," said Hlaka. Though whether he meant that they or the barber were adopting the right course, the barber did not know.

"Then," said the barber, "they will come up the mountain wherever there are none of your men, and cut the mountain in two, and bring up the men that are surrounding the empty part to strengthen the line surrounding the part where you are. And they will have a tank on the road, to prevent you getting to the lower slopes. And they hope to seize all the springs without any fighting, because they think you are above the springs. Then they will not lose a lot of men in attacking you, as they did last time, because you will have to attack them. They know how difficult it is to attack men lying down on the Mountain."

"How do you know all this?" said Hlaka.

"Alas," said the barber, "I am poor, it is my métier. How can I support myself, and a family of four children, with cutting hair and shaving in a small street and trimming a few beards, and sometimes, God knows how rarely, a shampoo, and that is only sixpence. God gave me two ears and I listen to talk. And He gave me a memory. That is all. Would you starve in a garden full of fruit? What I hear in my shop keeps me from starving. My family and I would have starved ere now without it. Once I heard a man say that he saw a man with a walking-stick and a particular kind of hat and wearing a tie of certain colours walk down a certain street. I chanced to remember the description of the man: my memory is like that, and I passed the information on, as most men do with most things that they hear. I described the man's tie exactly. And the man to whom I described it paid me money that kept me and my family for a whole day, and in comfort, and with wine for me in the evening. Was there harm in describing a tie that a man wore? Is there military significance in a necktie?"

"Did he escape alive?" asked Hlaka.

"What? Who?" said the barber.

"The Englishman," replied Hlaka.

"It was before the Germans entered," said the barber. "I think he escaped."

"And now," said Hlaka, "it is your own life that is in peril."

"Chieftain," said the barber, "I have told you everything."

"Tell me more," said Hlaka.

"I know no more," said the barber.

"When will they surround the Mountain?" said Hlaka.

"God knows," said the barber. "But they expect me back tomorrow night."

"In the morning you would have told them all you had spied," said Hlaka.

"I would tell them perhaps what I saw in the Mountain," said the barber, "like any man who goes for a long walk."

"And they would march the same day," said Hlaka.

"Perhaps the following day," said the spy.

"Who sent you?" asked Hlaka.

"Major von Wald," said the barber.

"I believe you speak the truth," said Hlaka.

"As God is over us I do," said the barber.

"Then you shall have your life," said Hlaka. And the barber knelt to thank him.

"At a price," added Hlaka.

"Master, at any price," said the spy.

"We have an account to settle with Major von Wald,"

said Hlaka. "Pay Major von Wald for us, and you shall live."

"With . . . with the knife?" asked the barber.

"With the knife," said Hlaka. "His blood or yours."

"How will I do it?" asked the barber.

"It is not difficult," said Hlaka. "As I told you, I have sixty-one men. They all know you, and you know Major von Wald. They know where you are to be found, and you know where he is to be found. You cannot both live. It may be," said Hlaka, "that others will have settled what we owe to Major von Wald before you find him. In that case you will pay in some other currency. But you are worth Major von Wald."

"I am honoured," said the barber.

"One villain for another villain," said Hlaka. "Go." And he pointed to where some of his mountaineers were watching a little way off.

The barber went back, smiling, to the men that were watching him. What Hlaka had said to him may have been hard; but he had heard hard words before and, besides that, he had not a very high opinion of men, and did not therefore set much store by their words. On the other hand his life, which for some moments had seemed in great peril, was, at least for the present, safe. As for Major von Wald, the matter might not be too difficult to arrange. The barber had an ingratiating manner, and he thought he might either approach him within reach of his heart, some time when he was alone, or even obtain his protection against all Hlaka's

men. For a moment he thought of shaving, and of luring
the major to his shop; but his shop was too public a place,
and he dismissed that thought at once. If he could get to
Germany—mighty Germany, that held all Europe in her
tremendous grasp—he would be safe from Hlaka and all his
men. And yet, turning over in his mind and rummaging
through the immense store of a spy's information, amongst
the dust of his memory, some little flashes twinkling amongst
its layers seemed to warn him, what even some statesmen
did not then know for certain, that of this mighty power in
a few years time there might be left no more than is left
today of the Colossus of Rhodes. These were the thoughts
of the barber as he walked to the group of armed men,
some of whom were henceforth to watch him until Hlaka
should decide that he could be safely sent to the city to
purchase his life with that of Major von Wald.

XVI

HAVING got his information, Hlaka turned to supplies. He
called for the cook, and asked him how much food the new
men had brought, and what he still had in the store. Little
was left. Nor was their supply of water large enough to last
more than three or four days, if the Germans were to cut
them off from the streams. His position high on the rocky

crags was good for fighting against men climbing up, but impossible to defend against a siege.

Hlaka now had ample ammunition, not for infantry fighting in any campaign such as has been fought in the last two hundred years, but enough for the warfare in which he was engaged, in which no volleys were fired, and each shot was fired close and accurately, for none of his men dared waste bullets. Hlaka's need was for marksmen and, though he had no hope of making a marksman in two days out of a man who could not shoot, he counted on training good fighting material, even in so short a time, to be able to hit a soldier at eighty yards, advancing not like a hunter, but like a drilled man in unfamiliar country.

The material he had was the men of a race that had had some familiarity for three thousand years with the instruments of music and battle. In those mountains a flute might sound at any time, or a note from the twang of a string would send a touch of mystery through the twilight; and if you searched on those mountains for the musician you would not find a maestro, nor anybody that was even taught by one; you would find a shepherd, or a boy herding goats, dressed for the mountains; yet they had the ear all right. Or show a good rifle to any of those men, and there comes that light in his eyes at once that you see amongst connoisseurs when some ancient and beautiful piece of china is shown to them, or some rare carving in jade or an exquisite etching. Weapons and song had been known so long by this people that, if you put into the hands of one of them an instrument of war or of melody, his fingers flickered about it waiting to be taught, if he did not well know the way of it already. There might be some among them that knew neither the knack of war nor of music; there might even be one, among hundreds, who had no longings reaching out to either of those ways; but such a man would not have gone up from spring almost to winter, from the comfort of houses to rocks and the open stars, from safety to such a war.

Hlaka ordered now that one-half of their ammunition was to be used, if necessary, to train the men till they could hit a match-box at eighty yards and hide themselves from the sight of a man at that distance.

Though Hlaka's first need was the need of marksmen, he knew the ingredients of war, and had no thought of waging it with any one of them missing. Therefore he ordered one of his men to go down to a farm he knew, the highest one in the Mountain, and to drive up the whole flock of sheep that the farmer had: there were only twenty, but Hlaka estimated that they would keep his men for more than a week.

This farmer had so far eluded the suspicions of the Germans, who believed that he only cared for a peaceful life and cared no more for the fortunes of his country or the fate of the world than to leave them in the hands of the *Herrenvolk*. But all he really cared for was liberty, and he looked to see Hlaka one day free The Land. Whatever he had that Hlaka wanted he gave: all he asked was that when his sheep should be required they should be driven off by armed men.

Other men Hlaka sent down the mountain road to a culvert through which a rivulet ran, carrying bags of gun-cotton. Hlaka had also amongst his stores a small electric battery and a hundred yards or so of wire. This party were to conceal the gun-cotton in the culvert, and find a place of concealment for the man who would work the electric battery.

And another man Hlaka sent down the Mountain into the plain to the north, to make his way to another farm and to bring from it four mules as soon as the dusk had fallen. On these four mules this man and the three women were to travel all night to the north. There they would find shelter in a house forty miles away, and go on the next night and find shelter again. No house was named. They had a very simple pass-word: it was *Heil Hitler;* and, if when the answer was given the "r" was rolled at the end, then all was well and the mountaineer only had to say "In the name of Hlaka." And, after that, all would be done that could be done for honoured guests in a household of a naturally hospitable people.

While Hlaka was making his plans and giving orders, Srebnitz walked with Gregor among the bare rocks of those peaks. It was good land for fighting; that is to say, for those that fought high up, against men who climbed from below. But it was bad land in which to live, land to which the wild sheep went, not because they liked bare mountain, but because they feared men: they would have chosen the green lawns, had they had the choice. And now Liberty walked in the lands that the wild sheep knew, because the green plains of Europe were not for them or her. Very far off to the north, they saw the line of another range of mountains, a paler blue than the sky.

Gregor asked Srebnitz about the fight in the house, and Srebnitz began to tell him, but very soon he drifted away from the subject. "Sophia," he said. "You saw her."

"Yes," said Gregor.

"She is very beautiful," said Srebnitz.

"Yes," Gregor replied.

He wanted to tell Gregor how beautiful, but the right words would not come; so he sighed and turned to another subject: "Why did the Germans want to accuse her aunts?" he asked.

"Because they found out," said Gregor. "Some spy must have told them."

"Told them what?" asked Srebnitz.

"That they are Hlaka's sisters."

"Hlaka's sisters!" exclaimed Srebnitz.

The old ladies with their knitting and easy chairs in the comfortable, tidy room. Was that the blood that led the mountaineers, and defied the whole might of Germany? He thought for a moment. Then he saw that it was. Their quiet calm house, their serene faces, their garden and the old fruit-trees, their Dresden china, German though it was, and their old and orderly ways—all these things must be against Hitler; and if he roused such blood to fight, might he not call up such a figure as Hlaka, to defend gardens and quiet rooms to the last, even on the bare Mountain? Yes, he saw now that their brother might be such as Hlaka. And then another thought surged into his mind.

"Then Sophia?" he blurted out.

"She is his daughter," said Gregor.

"Oh, yes," said Srebnitz, trying to conceal his astonishment.

And Gregor said something about Sophia's mother, who had died long ago, a woman of the mountains they could dimly see to the north; but Srebnitz, with his mind flashing with new visions of Sophia, never heard what he said. No scientist had taught him that all the metals in the sun are to be found in Earth and her sister planets, but some instinct surer than science had given him a glimpse of the unity of Creation, so that he often saw some trivial event of his everyday life mirrored in stars or mountains; and he suddenly thought now of a day when he had first gone to the grey crags of the Mountain and found, where there was no grass and scarcely soil, a pink rock-rose upon a precipice. And it had for a moment surprised him, as it surprised him now to hear that the fair and slender Sophia was the daughter of rugged Hlaka.

XVII

AT ABOUT sunset the mountaineers moved along the Mountain some way from their caves, and there prepared a big fire out of oak-scrub to cook their supper and to keep them warm and cheerful while they ate it; for they still had enough provisions left for a meal of meat. There they all gathered, and there Isabella, Angelica and Sophia sat near Hlaka on a heap of blankets.

Srebnitz was anxious lest a shell should come while Sophia was there, for the fire was sending up a large column of smoke, and even the light of it began to glow as the twilight faded away, which it does so soon in that latitude. But looking at the others he soon saw that they were content, noticing that they trusted in Hlaka; and it was evident that, whether from experience or prophecy, Hlaka knew that the German guns were not going to fire that night. Indeed they never enquired how Hlaka got his knowledge: it was enough for them that he knew. And one may mention that what Hlaka knew was a very simple piece of knowledge: he had their spy with him and the spy was expected to stay till the following evening, and the Germans would not shoot at their own spy, unless they had something special to gain by it.

Only two men knew, besides Hlaka, that the barber was a spy, and he did not know that they knew. They sat near him and had their rifles, but they pretended that they were on watch for aeroplanes. All the rest of the mountaineers treated him as a comrade, and so did the two men that knew.

With the fire between him and Hlaka, and the men about him talking cheerfully to him, the barber's spirits soon rose from any depth to which Hlaka may have downcast them, and he talked and listened as he was wont to talk and listen

in the shop where he plied his two trades. At the height of
his mirth one of his two guards turned to a man by his side
and asked him to bring from their stores a bottle of a certain wine made only on one small island, a wine much treasured by the people of that land; and the man who went to
get it wondered that so much honour was to be paid to the
latest member of their band. But the man who guarded him
saw that the wine that he had already had loosened the locks
on his lips and that this rare vintage would open them wide
and recklessly.

The bottle was brought and the drinking-horn of the spy
was filled with wine, and he drank and became still merrier.
And, when he was humming a song, his two guards brought
him before Hlaka, hoping for more information. But the
face of Hlaka in the firelight suddenly sobered him. And
he said that he was a poor man, and unworthy to speak with
the chieftain. And they led him away from Hlaka to the
other side of the fire, and sat near, watching him.

Had a man passed that camp-fire and noticed all the men
that were gathered about it, but without the glance that ob-
serves deeply, he might have reported that the happiest man
in the group was the barber and that the saddest was Srebnitz. And indeed his report might have been true, for there
is an exhilaration about the presence of Death, and the barber had been very near him; whereas the shining peaks of
love overlook abysses, in the shadows of which the hopes of
Srebnitz were wandering, as he saw the preparations now
being made for Sophia's long journey. He did not know

when they would meet again. He did not know how she would welcome him if ever they did, and he wished to speak with her so as to get some clue, but he could not lead her away from the terrible Hlaka. It was Sophia herself that gave him the opportunity that he had thought was lost; when, just as she and her aunts were leaving the fire, having said farewell to Hlaka, she pitied the man that was to accompany them, because of all the baggage he had to carry; and, looking over her shoulder as though at random, to speak to the nearest man, her glance fell upon Srebnitz.

"Help him to carry some of those blankets, please," said Sophia. "He'll never be able to manage so many."

The man protested that he could easily carry the blankets; but Srebnitz came, and carried one of the blankets down the Mountain towards where the mules were waiting.

"Don't hurry," said Sophia, "you have so much to carry."

And this was true in a way, for Srebnitz had his rifle as well as the blanket; and the light was leaving the rocks, so that fast walking was difficult. And besides that, thought Srebnitz, Sophia cannot have noticed exactly what I am carrying. So he went slowly, as she told him, walking last of all. And presently Sophia dropped back a little behind her aunts. Isabella glanced round at her, but after all said nothing. As they came to the line at which they first saw moths flying, and they were past the bare rocks, and shrubs began to appear, Sophia was walking with Srebnitz.

"The chieftain is your father," said Srebnitz.

A momentary look, almost of alarm, crossed Sophia's

face, as though she had learned to fear such a statement. But the Mountain was all round her now, and she smiled. "Yes," she said, "but never mention that anywhere outside the Mountain."

"Why not?" asked Srebnitz.

"Reprisals," answered Sophia.

"Did they know when they came to your house?" asked Srebnitz.

"They suspected," said Sophia. "And they wanted to make my aunts confess."

They walked in silence awhile, for Srebnitz was a little awed by knowing that Sophia was the daughter of that Consort of Liberty, and that she was of the royal blood of the Mountain.

Sadness prolonged their silence. Sophia was sad because she knew that as she went down that slope she went to a land enslaved, and upon Srebnitz the coming parting with Sophia weighed heavily.

Then the mountaineers sang by their fire on the height, one of the ballads of that ancient people, and the song reached to them, welling over the Mountain; and, though they could not distinguish the syllables, they knew the simple words. Indeed the words were too simple to show forth in print, to dare to challenge the gaze of a reader's eyes, and it is probable that they had never been written down. They were something about a goat that was lost from the herd, and about a young goatherd who searched for it; but without the accompanying music on the stringed instruments of that land, and the note of the horn of the goatherd, there is really nothing to say of it. And yet it called up for Srebnitz and Sophia echoes out of the vast of lost ages, and brought a voice as of The Land itself, babbling perhaps in infancy, from over the heave of the years, that spoke from the days when all their people were free, to those that were free still, though only upon that mountain.

To Sophia there was all the romance about Srebnitz of one who helped to guard the liberty that The Land had had for ages; and somehow she found another glow that illumined him, from no deed of his own, but from hers; for she had helped him on his way when he was lost and pursued, on the night that they first met; and this too cast upon him some of the enchantment that we mean by the word romance.

She to him was nothing to be so logically described, but he thought of her, and remembered her long after, as so clearly associated with the grandeur of the crags, and with the beauty of leaves and flowers and wandering moths, so mingled with the last of the twilight that shone in the sky and dimly gleamed on her face, that it might be said that his memories gazed towards her as to an incarnation of the Mountain. Its rocky slopes did not seem too harsh for the grace of Sophia, for he thought of the wild beauty of the flowers that they put forth; and, whether he knew it or not, there was a tenderness in the grim Hlaka's fierce love for The Land, that had blossomed in the beauty of Sophia.

Their talk was of trivial things, the mere words trivial as

the words of the song that they heard above them ringing down the ages; yet those words would have told of time-outlasting things, if they could have spoken aright of the vision of those two minds, which saw the future as a glittering land where roads ran golden with sunlight, and the past as a splendid gloom that romance had illumined, while the present shone between them in an enchanted glory.

When planets shone, and one or two of the stars, and a glimmer of light was still in the western sky, they came where, on the rough feet of the mountain, two of Hlaka's men were waiting with the four mules.

As Srebnitz heard the stir of the hooves that moved as the long ears caught the sound of feet on the mountain, Srebnitz knew that the long story of his days with Sophia was over, until some time far from his knowledge. The long story. How many days was it? How many hours? But Srebnitz did not count it in days or hours. The years of his life had run smoothly, with new experience gradually opening before him, as his boyhood grew to maturity. And suddenly manhood had come to him like an avalanche; when, instead of being cared for by his father and mother, and guided by the laws and ways of his country, he saw his parents led away, not to return, and he had to save his country, whose laws were lost. In such a time there had flashed on him the beauty of Sophia, shining in the midst of disaster; and events had followed of a magnitude and with a rapidity that so crowded his days, that they were not to be compared with the events of his other days, but rather matched, in the making of the destiny of Srebnitz, the events of as many of his years. In his memory one of the days since the Germans came loomed as large as that; and it may well be that in his life the time of those three or four days was condensed or intensified in such a way as to make it the equal of two or three idle years. This we can never know, since we have no way of measuring time, except by the ticking of clocks and the movement of sun and stars. There are, or have been, alchemists with the power to condense time, showing that, like air and unlike water, it has the property of being able to be so treated. Aeschylus, Euripides, Sophocles, Aristophanes and Shakespeare were some of these: they condensed and intensified the events of lifetimes, so that anyone watching a piece of the work of any of these for a few hours would see and feel, with jubilance or in sorrow, but in either case profoundly, as much of the way of man, and the behaviour towards him of Destiny, as they would see in reading the most careful record of the whole life of many a man of their own time and country. And there is another besides those I have mentioned who illuminates man's story and intensifies hours and days with the same tremendous power that these had, one whom four of them called Ares and the fifth called Mars.

In times thus enchanted, and among terrible splendours, moved Srebnitz to his meeting with Sophia. He did not feel his emotions as men feel them who walk calmly down pavements in times of peace, and he did not count the days that he had known her as the days that they mark on almanacks, but rather as the people in a theatre count time, while a lifetime passes before them in an evening. And it seemed a long, long story.

And what of Sophia's feelings? She was silent as they went down the last of the slope; she mounted a mule; Isabella and Angelica mounted too, and the mountaineer that was to accompany them. Hlaka's men let go of the bridles, and Sophia with a quick movement kissed her hand to Srebnitz. Isabella turned her head as quickly upon Sophia, and was about to speak, when the two mountaineers that had been holding the mules took off their hats and bowed low to her and Angelica and kissed a hand to each.

"Is all the world going mad?" said Isabella.

Angelica sighed and answered, "Perhaps."

And in the light of that information it seemed that Isabella decided to humour it, and kissed her hand to the man who had kissed his to her. And Angelica, before the darkness quite hid her, did the same as her sister.

From the sorrowful border between plain and mountain where the parting had been, Srebnitz and the two mountaineers climbed back to the hospitality of the crags.

XVIII

When Srebnitz and the two mountaineers got back to the point from which they had started red embers were still glowing, and still no shell had been fired at them. But Hlaka and all his men had left, and gone back to their caves. Thither the three men followed.

It may have been from the sadness of his mind, overcast by his parting from Sophia, that the thought arose, or it may be that the waterless slope he trod brought a plain truth close to his eyes; but, whatever its origin, Srebnitz for the first time felt doubt. To fight with sixty-one men against five thousand, in country of which the enemy would know nothing, seemed not impossible when led by Hlaka; but three things go to the making of black gunpowder, and a few more to the making of war, and one of these was water; and it was very clear that those peaks could not be held long. And then into the sadness of Srebnitz's mind there came insidiously, like deadly insects to marshes, the words of the traitor that had made his speech in the market-place on the day the Germans marched in: they could not fight against tanks in the plains. The oak-scrub and the myrtle between the two, where water was to be had, Hlaka had for some reason abandoned; no one knew why, for he never discussed his plans, but made them from his experience of past years and whatever that may have taught him of the future.

"What shall we do for water?" asked Srebnitz of one of the two men that were with him.

"Hlaka will see to that," said the man, and something in his tone warned Srebnitz that his doubt was being detected; and doubts about leaders are useless, for victory will not come to doubting followers if the leader is right, and if he

is wrong they are all lost in any case. No one else could lead
this little band against the German forces: it was Hlaka or
nothing, and Srebnitz said no more. But still the doubt per-
sisted. Did it come to Srebnitz from sadness? Did sadness raise phantoms before his eyes? Or did it brighten
them to see more clearly a truth that should already be clear
enough? Srebnitz never knew.

He went on in silence till they came to the caves. Tired,
in the late night, some miles from civilisation, there came
on Srebnitz a feeling he often felt in those days with
Hlaka, though he never expressed it in words, a feeling of
home close to him just when he needed it most, the sudden
comfortable realisation that the rocks and the stars, the dark
peaks of the Mountain and the crisp night air, were what
roof and walls are to less free men.

He went to the cave in which his blankets were, and
wrapped them both round him and lay down. A small sack
made him a pillow, and he kept on his boots, not in order
to be instantly ready, but merely because the slight increase
of comfort he might have obtained by removing them was
one of the trifles out of a past life which he forgot on the
Mountain, as he seemed to come closer to eternal things such
as the stars and liberty. A cold wind running into the cave
and searching amongst its nooks, something he once would
have looked upon as a draught and as being annoying and
hostile, was now to him more like a neighbour, a friendly
spirit resident in the Mountain: he felt it passing over his
hands and face, and heard its low whisperings for a little
while, and very soon was asleep.

He was called in the morning by Aurora herself, for his cave faced to the east, and as soon as the sun leapt up the whole of the camp was awake. There was no matter of clocks here: as soon as the sun was risen the day had started: the day was part of their life, and they started with it.

Hlaka was already out on the Mountain, where he had long been inspecting the rocks. Gregor and Iskander came by the cave and called to Srebnitz, who walked with them to the place among the rocks at which they were to have breakfast, which had been cooked over a fire nearly a mile away. The sheep had arrived during the night, as Gregor told Srebnitz, and three or four had been killed and the rest hidden in a cave. Srebnitz heard no sound of them, and wondered in what cave they were hidden. But Gregor stopped his questionings. It seemed that such things were not to be talked about. In reality the bulk of the flock had gone down the Mountain, and was taken northward all night by one of the new members of Hlaka's band who, true though he was to the cause of liberty and of Europe, was not able to be brought up in so short a time as there was to spare to Hlaka's standard for marksmen.

In a small ravine they all breakfasted, while one sentry watched, without a bayonet or even a rifle: he watched only with his ears, at an instrument that could hear aeroplanes at a great distance. No evil thing having yet befallen the spy, the relief so exalted him that his spirits were the highest of any one of the band.

On Hlaka's face, when he returned from the rocks, there was no expression but one, which seemed to hide from all the men around him a personality sunk deep in thought. After breakfast he beckoned to the spy, and walked a little way with him, and when they were out of hearing of the rest Hlaka said: "Your friends expect you this evening, so we must lose you. There are few things you can tell them about me that they will wish to know. But if you tell them any of those . . ."

"I will tell them nothing, master," said the spy.

"Perhaps not," said Hlaka. "There are men that have told them about my movements; but you will not meet those men."

"I do not keep such company, master," the barber answered.

"You will keep such company," said Hlaka, "if you tell them what I do not wish to be known."

"Never, master."

Hlaka said nothing and a fear came over the barber, a mere hint of it, like the chill from one waif of a wing of Fear. And he said: "Where are they, master?"

"They are all dead," said Hlaka.

A silence fell on the barber.

"Your name," said Hlaka, "is Trigoloutros; your shop is 44 in the Street of the Martyrs; and we can find you at any time."

"I know what I have to do," said Trigoloutros.

"That is well," said Hlaka, and returned to his men.

Left alone, the spy loitered about the rocks for a while as though undecided whether to wait to return till the hour

that his masters expected him, or whether to accept at once
what seemed like Hlaka's dismissal. He glanced at the
figure of Hlaka going back to the caves, and took a step in his
direction, then suddenly turned and went the other way.
And those that watched the road during the morning saw
him walking out of the Mountain towards the town.

All day Hlaka continued his preparations, as he seemed
to have done all the night, for no one saw Hlaka sleep. At
the same time that he chose and examined his battlefield he
superintended the drill of his recruits, or what stood them
instead of drill, which was to learn to go unseen and to
shoot with moderate accuracy at short ranges. No march
past of the most splendid troops in the world would have
pleased Hlaka so much as a march past, through rocks and
myrtle, that was invisible from the saluting-base. At the
same time he sent men to draw such stores as he needed
from what may be called his depots. For it was only to the
superficial eye that Hlaka appeared to be without commissariat, and Hlaka drew his food and stores as he needed them
from his depots as regularly as any leader in the field, even
if the men of his commissariat moved irregularly, and even
surreptitiously, to the farms that held his stores. No forms
had to be filled in, no accounts kept by a quartermaster:
what Hlaka needed was given him by the whole country, in
return for which he was one day to give liberty to The Land.
Three or four ropes twenty yards long were what some of
his men were now seeking among the farms below the Mountain. The peaks towards the city went down among bare

grey rocks with a great sweep like those of draperies, till they came to the oak-scrub and myrtle and then to the heaths; but to the northward there were amongst the slopes some belts of rock that were sheer.

About halfway down the Mountain on that side one of these precipices ran for a few hundred yards without any gap or cleft cut by avalanche or water, and was fifty or sixty feet high. A few pine-trees crowned the top of it. It was not for defence that Hlaka had chosen this precipice, for no defence was needed on that part of the Mountain, since no one could climb the precipice, or, if he did, would be choosing the most difficult part of the slope and would waste the time of the whole attack, if the rest were compelled to keep pace with him. Equally difficult it was to descend, and for this reason Hlaka chose it for his line of retreat, when the time should come for retreating. No one would expect him to retire over a sixty-foot precipice, and it was here that he tied his ropes to the trunks of the pine-trees and coiled them up into heaps at the butts of the trees. That was to the north of the crags, where the far blue mountains could be seen shining faintly.

To Srebnitz and the men who had joined Hlaka before him he explained what he meant to do, and what the Germans would do. "We shall crush them with numbers," he said. A curious remark from a man who was about to fight with sixty-one men against five thousand, and yet he was right enough, for on a terrain that he knew well, wherever he moved his men they would be overwhelmingly superior to part of a line that was surrounding a mountain. Had he been able to find water at that altitude he would have probably held out among those peaks for as long as the war lasted. Amongst the myrtle and heath, where the water was, Hlaka had decided that he could not hold out indefinitely, because the Germans could have taken the peaks and fired down on him, while others came up from below: Hlaka did not tell his men this, for he did not discuss his plans with them, but that was the reason he had gone to the higher ground above the springs of the streams. Then Hlaka stood and gazed at the far blue mountains, till his men wondered if he meant to make so great a journey through land that the enemy held.

"But are they in The Land?" asked one of them.

For it is a small country and, though the nearer peaks of the blue mountains were inside its borders, a part of the range ran into other lands.

"There are no frontiers any longer," said Hlaka. "It matters nothing whether we are in our own Land or in lands that are for us, or even in those that are for the enemy. Where there are mountains, there will be free men. But there are no more frontiers."

"How shall we get there, Chieftain?" asked one of his men.

"The wild sheep went," replied Hlaka, and deigned to say nothing more to explain how men should do what sheep had done.

XIX

WHEN Hlaka and his men came over the crags to the rocky slope on which they were camped, far below which lay the city, they saw a sight infrequent upon that mountain in times of peace and still rarer in time of war, for a taxi was coming up the mountain road. Hlaka's sentries, lying behind rocks with their rifles, watched it with curiosity. Before it got to the end of the road it stopped and a man got out, whom even at that distance they recognized as Trigoloutros by his slinking gait. He walked on up the rest of the road and started climbing the bare slope towards them among the large rocks, while the taxi began to turn and, when it had done that, waited. Trigoloutros saw no one as he climbed; but, when he was about in the midst of Hlaka's force, one of them came up to him and led him to Hlaka. Hlaka was sitting now in front of his cave on a pile of sacks.

"Master," said Trigoloutros, "I have found something that you would wish to know, and have come to tell you."

"How did you get the taxi?" asked Hlaka.

The spy looked towards it in a surprised way, as though he wondered too. "I hailed it," he said, "and asked the man to drive me up to your Excellency."

"How do you know what news I wish to hear?" asked Hlaka.

"Master," said Trigoloutros, "it is my métier to know such things. And I hoped to please you by coming at once."

"What is your news?" said Hlaka.

"They will execute the Bishop of Ilion at dawn tomorrow," the spy said.

"Where is he now?" said Hlaka.

"In the prison," said Trigoloutros.

"Where will they execute him?"

"By the execution wall in the pine-wood," said the spy.

"You must go to von Wald," said Hlaka, "and tell him that we are coming to rescue the Bishop at dawn."

"Tell him that you are coming?" said the spy.

"All of us," said Hlaka. "And then you may say to him what you will. You barbers can talk. But, whatever you say, he must give the order for the Bishop to be executed at once instead of at dawn. That will be about midnight, when you go to see the major. Some of us will be there, behind the wall in the pine-wood. They will bring the Bishop to the wall with the firing-party in front of it. The Germans will expect one volley, and one volley there will be; and that will be the last play of that sort, or of any sort, that will be seen by that firing-party. Be sure that you do not fail with Major von Wald. For if the Bishop dies . . ." and Hlaka gave one look at the spy and saw that further words were not needed.

"I will do my best, master," said Trigoloutros.

Hlaka said nothing.

The pine-wood to which the spy referred was one that

came right into the town and to the very wall of the prison. Cities have strange things in them; Constantine in Algeria has a profound ravine, Bristol and Dublin have the sea, Edinburgh has a precipice, and there are paved streets that suddenly turn up a mountain; indeed cities have many surprises: this one has a small forest.

"I will do my best, master," Trigoloutros said again.

Hlaka gave him another look, but did not speak. And the look suddenly awoke so much fear in the spy, that his wiles were all awakened from the lairs in which they slept lightly in the hidden dark of his brain, and he pondered cunningly how to lure Major von Wald to give the fatal order that should save the Bishop of Ilion. He smiled at Hlaka, hoping to placate him, for Hlaka's look still frightened him; but the look froze his smile, and he saw that there was nothing for it but to do as he had been told.

"I will do it, master," said Trigoloutros.

Hlaka nodded. And the spy turned to go. Before he went Hlaka said: "Do not get von Wald's order till you see a fire here on the Mountain. Watch the Mountain. When the fire is lit we shall be ready."

"I will watch, master," said Trigoloutros.

Hlaka said no more, and the spy went down the rocks towards the road and his taxi.

Then Hlaka called to Srebnitz, Iskander and Gregor, and the cook, and three more of his best shots, and they all had a meal together before the rest, while Hlaka told them his plan.

They were to march, as Hlaka's army marched, not in fours but in ones, not by their right or by their left, but each man guiding himself; not marching upright, but slipping from doorpost to doorpost, running in bare feet on pavement, hiding in gardens, and then running on again: they were to take dark blankets, and wear them as cloaks, with their rifles under their cloaks, and each man must have his knife in his hand, but lying hidden along the arm. They were to meet in the pine-wood behind the low white wall, in front of which Hitler's men carried out their executions. A little outside the edge of the town where a few fruit-trees stood amidst open country, nearly the whole of the rest of Hlaka's force would wait, so that, if they had to fight their way back, they would not have far to go before they could outnumber any pursuers.

They were ready as soon as twilight touched the Mountain. And, as soon as the light from the sunset was dimmer than that of the moon, the eight men moved down the slope through myrtle and heath, aiming for a part of the town a long way to the left of the end through which they had come before, that is to say to the east. Birds were flying back to the trees as they went, and bats were about before they came to the town. They were moving through light by which men could not be seen at a distance.

As they came nearer the town the night came with them, and they moved among shadows, less visible than the moths that rose from the heath they disturbed, to sail upon swift pale wings that gleamed in the moonlight. When they were

close to the town's edge there was that touch of blue on white
walls that is part of the moon's enchantment. All was quiet
in the town amongst whose municipal by-laws was one that
imposed death for being out after sunset, except for the
enemy, the boots of whose patrols sounded now and again
through the stillness.

It was a little city, although a capital, perhaps not greatly
larger than Canterbury. Two or three small streets were all
they had to cross before they came to the little forest that lay
in the heart of the town. A black cat stole into the town down
a little street, heard marching feet in front and stopped to
listen, and slipped into a garden among magnolias and
lemon-trees: Gregor, whose dark shape, with bare feet,
moved also along that street, did the same as the cat had
done. And Srebnitz, who was a few yards away, copied
Gregor. When the street was hushed again, all three ran
on.

To anyone watching from a window of that street the night
would have seemed full of shadows, as does any moonlit
night; and amongst those shadows were Hlaka and the rest
of his eight men. All of them came, unseen by any German,
to the pine-wood that, so strangely in a city, sheltered Nature
even by day, and by night was such a place as might harbour
yet, so far as one could imagine, whatever ancient spirits had
ever blessed The Land; and wanderers in that wood when the
world was at peace felt they were nearer to things that
lurked at the edge of their understanding, and were nearer
to unknown shapes that the poets had seen, than most people
in other cities may hope to come. Right up to the very walls

the forest came, as though Nature here were not afraid of man, nor man hostile to Nature. The little white-washed wall, barely five feet high and built of rounded stones, that ran into it for a little way and then stopped as though lost in the forest, was not sophisticated enough to jar on the calm of the pines, and looked as though it could never scare a dryad. It was against this wall that the Germans were accustomed to place any men or women that they desired to execute.

Hlaka had signalled with an electric torch to men behind him just before he came to the pines, and they had flashed the signal on to the Mountain and a fire was burning now on one of the peaks. Hlaka drew up his men shoulder to shoulder along the wall on the far side from the prison, and stole softly away through the wood like a creature of fable. Softly he slipped out into the streets of the town, and came to the street in which Srebnitz's parents had lived.

There he waited listening, ready to hide if a patrol should come, but expecting another step. And the other step was heard. It was the barber. And he passed by Hlaka in the dark without seeing him, as men often went by Hlaka. And Hlaka put his left hand over the barber's mouth, and rapped his right hand above his heart, and whispered in his ear, "It will be like that, if . . ." And when he lifted his left hand, and the barber could breathe again, and was about to protest that never would he betray Hlaka, Hlaka said "Hush," and slipped back among shadows again, and returned to his men in the forest.

There are men whom those in high places receive at any

time; for those in high places cannot choose with whom they will associate, as easily as others can choose. Trigoloutros was always sure of being received by such. He knocked on the door of the house that had been Srebnitz's home, two quick light knocks followed by two heavy slow ones, and the door was opened at once, and the spy slunk in.

"Master," said Trigoloutros, "the disaffected men, the bandits, have found out about the Bishop, and they will rescue him at dawn with their whole force, unless . . ."

"Unless?" said the major.

"Unless they should be forestalled," said the spy. "They believe the execution will be at dawn."

"So it will," said the major.

"Then they will rescue him," said the spy.

"By what road will they come?" said Major von Wald.

"Master, one cannot tell with Hlaka's men," said the spy. "But they will come at dawn."

"Is this true?" said the major.

"Master, I swear it is true," said the spy. "How should I lie to so important an officer, when a few hours will reveal everything? If Hlaka's men are not soon on their way from the Mountain I have lied to you, master, and do not deserve to live. If Hlaka's men do not come you will know. How should I dare to lie?"

"I will send out men to stop them," said the major, and his hand went to a telephone that was now in the room.

"Master," said Trigoloutros so plaintively, and so appealingly stretching out his hands, that the major turned to him and did not lift the receiver, "they will slip round in the dark. We cannot tell by what way they will come. By daylight they could never get back, if they waited by the execution-wall and the Bishop did not come."

The major paused and was silent, and did not lift the receiver. When Trigoloutros saw that he had got the idea he said no more and left it all to the major, who presently lifted the receiver and got on to the prison and said: "Let the Bishop be executed at once."

That was all. And Trigoloutros began to protest again that the coming of Hlaka and his men to the town would prove that he spoke the truth, as he always did, at any rate to the Germans. But those that have the entrée to high places for such reasons as passed-in the barber, stay in such places no longer than their enchantment is able to work. The enchantment was the information he brought and, this having been given, there was no more welcome for Trigoloutros; so he tried to smile, and he made a bow, and was soon shown out, and went back to his shop holding a pass in his hand which entitled him to be in the streets at night, and live.

XX

DMITRIPOULOS, titular Bishop of Ilion, had been arrested the day before and tried that morning by a German court-martial that had sentenced him to death.

The Bishop had not entirely understood the charges, but there was no doubt that he was guilty. He had the idea that he received his orders only from the head of his Church, and that the head of his Church was a higher power even than Hitler. Consequently all orders he received from the Germans, although heard with the utmost politeness, were, if they clashed with the ritual or discipline of his church, invariably ignored. So it was not long before a German sergeant and two soldiers with fixed bayonets had called at the Bishop's house, and were smilingly received by the Bishop, whom they marched off to prison. From this he was brought next day before the court-martial, to whose president he bowed, and then listened to a charge with a great many clauses, many of which appeared true.

The Bishop found it difficult to defend himself without impoliteness, and against some of the charges for this reason he made no defence whatever. But it is unlikely that his defence against these would have been more successful than the defence that he did make against the rest, and death was monotonously the penalty for each of them. There were twenty charges, and the court-martial found the Bishop guilty of all, and sentenced him to death; and he bowed again and was led away.

Back in his cell in the prison the Bishop reflected on many things. His thoughts, intensified by the nearness of death, looked keenly into the present, the past and the future. He saw vividly the strength of Germany in the present, and how armies, from a force amounting to millions, sent into small countries, could easily crush them and could hold them by the terrible methods such as he himself had experienced, which paralyzed the nerves of weaker men, leaving them helpless, while some that were weak and cunning were driven by fear actually to work for the terror that was oppressing them. Into the future he looked with singular clearness, perhaps scarcely to be expected in a man without military knowledge, and saw how the methods that made the Germans so powerful in the present would drive them forth like pariahs in the future from all lands, back to their own.

His thoughts, as they flitted backwards and forwards through time, swift as a butterfly caught in a net, saw Hitler as a colossus of granite, vaster than any image that Egyptian monarchs had left: he saw that colossus again a little while hence, a little further on through the years that he viewed, shattered by its fall and its own great weight, and lying broken so small that flowers came up through the pieces and the world grew fair again.

Then his thoughts turned from these things, from the dark present and from the ruin yet to come to the colossus that darkened it, and they looked only into the past, and to the beauty of The Land before the colossus came. These days were before Hitler had ever attacked Russia, and the Bishop can have had little to guide his insight into the future, unless it was sheer prophecy.

And now he turned to the past. He had very serene memories, and his thoughts travelled as brightly down them as winged things riding a sunbeam. They passed through dim churches in which small lamps glowed and flashes of light came from silver and gold in ikons, and out beyond into earlier days before he had been a priest, and even a long while before, back as far as scenes that till now he thought were forgotten.

The thoughts were simple and clear, and might be told, but not in one volume; for these last thoughts that ran swiftly over the years, looking down at the days of them from the altitude of his last hours, were more numerous than can be told of in one book, even by a pen that was able to do them justice. There was material there for many books and many poems. Indeed a writer searching for human thoughts rising up from the earth's surface, under which their roots go down beyond reach of the eye, is like a botanist looking for flowers on a prairie that goes far beyond the horizon: if he gather a few and bring them home unwithered, those he must leave ungathered, and even unseen, are in millions beyond computation. So the thoughts of the Bishop of Ilion on this day were more than could be gathered by any pen, and so far as we know are lost; but then we do not know.

Very early that afternoon such sunlight as came to his cell through the small barred window began to fade away, but no brightness passed from the scenes of his youth in gardens that he remembered; rather, in the dimmer light his inner vision strengthened, as if it had been a little dazzled by visible light, and he saw more clearly yet the light of the days long past. Alas that there must be many men in various lands, sitting thus in prison close to their last hour, with a German sentry outside.

Once the gaoler came in to bring the Bishop his dinner.
He was a compatriot of the Bishop, a native of The Land,
and had been gaoler there for years: when the Germans
came they employed him at his old work without question.
He had had no especial interest in the Germans, or much
knowledge of them, or of anything outside the city, but when
they came they took to each other at once. There seemed
something in his work and something in Hitler's, if one may
compare very small things with great, that were attuned to
each other; and so, although in a very humble way, he felt a
sympathy for the authority that had dominion of most of
Europe.

The Bishop asked him what time dawn would be, and this
the gaoler knew well, for he had lately called many of his
guests at an hour that got them ready in time for the dawn,
and he calculated roughly that it was two minutes later each
day. He told the Bishop, and the Bishop thanked him.

Then the gaoler went out with his keys and locked the
door, and the Bishop was left alone again with his memories:
like returning swallows seeing the eaves they knew, his memories crossed the years to red-tiled villages under the hills
of The Land and by the edge of old cork-forests, into whose
glades they went among the splendour of forests owing
nothing to man; and whether they flew to these glades or
through gardens that man had beautified, always there rose
at the edge of all scenes that his memory saw a distant pale-
blue line of wrinkled mountains, that seemed to be seated
gravely watching The Land as a summer's day went by, and
as the centuries crossed it. The sight of those mountains that

many years of gazing at them had left so clear in that vision that we call memory helped the Bishop to look more easily upon time than he could have looked at it with a finite mind, were his mind unaided by these mighty shapes that seemed to him to be somewhere midway between time and eternity. And the beauty of them seemed to promise well to his hopes; for, if they really stood between time and eternity, the beauty of this door at the end of time was full of promise of what might be beyond.

Sometimes among his thoughts a dark fear would glide, as to how it would be at dawn, shadowing and chilling these bright scenes for some moments, but there were serene spaces amongst his memories to which he was able to turn where these fears did not follow, and mostly these serene spaces lay under the blue mountains. And beyond those mountains, beyond The Land, beyond the world—what was there?

He had set aside much of the night for prayer, for he did not mean to sleep; and now evening was coming on, and with it darkness in the cell. In this darkness he saw past days with the greatest clearness; and it is here that the volumes were needed and the enchanted pen, if any justice were to be done to all the tales to be told, that he saw as he searched the past. Nor could the life of any man be told adequately without many volumes and an enchanted pen, for the thoughts of men are the material for poetry, wherever they can be seen and their swift flight overtaken.

At midnight the Bishop's meditations were disturbed by

the sound of the lock of his door, and the gaoler returned. He was almost a little shy, some decent sense revealing to him how much he intruded.

"It is to be tonight instead of at dawn," he said.

"When?" asked the Bishop.

"Now," said the gaoler.

"But that gives me no time for my prayers," said the Bishop.

The gaoler shrugged his shoulders and looked down at the floor. Then the steps of three men marching were heard in the passage outside.

"But I am not yet ready," said the Bishop.

The men marched in at that moment, a corporal and two other soldiers, and a glance at their faces showed to the Bishop of Ilion that no words of his could have any effect on them or even convey any meaning. And at the same moment he saw that the words were untrue: he was ready; he had always been ready. He would have liked to have said more prayers, but he would have liked many things which could not possibly thrive beneath the weight of what now crushed The Land. He saw in two flashes all these decent things crushed, and also some sort of essence arising up from their ruin, which should utterly overcome the force that now crushed them.

"I beg your pardon," he said. "I am ready."

And the corporal marched him away between the two men. Some sort of regret came to the gaoler, like a flower growing on rock; but it passed, like a flower withered. The prison gate was at the edge of the pine-wood and, when it was opened, three more soldiers joined them. There was an officer also, waiting outside, and while the three men fell in behind the Bishop the officer walked into the wood. The party went no more than forty yards, when the corporal halted them. Then he led the Bishop up to the white wall and began to blindfold him.

"What need in the dark?" said the Bishop.

But the corporal did not seem to understand. The firing-party were only a few yards away, on account of the darkness of the night, which would have made shooting difficult at more than a few yards. The men were in two ranks, with a space at the right of the rear rank for the corporal, to which he now went. The officer a little to the right of the firing-party had an electric torch, which he now turned on to the Bishop's chest, where a gold crucifix twinkled. And then he drew a breath to give an order, and the breath went out through his side, for at that moment Hlaka shot him. And the volley that the Germans, listening in the prison, expected to hear came from eight rifles instead of six, and was fired from over the wall instead of at it. One belated shot came after the rest, as in a badly fired volley: it was Hlaka shooting the sixth man, who alone had not dropped at once. For a moment Hlaka and his six men waited motionless, to see if any surprise had been caused to the Germans; but nothing stirred in the prison; the firing-party and their officer were past all surprises: nobody was surprised but the Bishop. Hlaka slipped over the wall and went up to him.

"It is Hlaka," he said in his ear. "The Germans are dead now." And he began to untie the bandage over his eyes, which was knotted over a little circle of plaited hair that the priests of the Orthodox church wear at the back.

"Thank you," said the Bishop.

"We must go to the Mountain," said Hlaka. "Would it be too much to ask you to take off your boots?"

XXI

More than anything Hlaka avoided firing at night in the town, on account of the great difficulty of getting away afterwards, and he forbade all his men to do it. But the volley tonight rather lulled than disturbed the Germans, for they had been warned by telephone to expect an execution at midnight. One senior officer was awakened from sleep by the single shot following the rest, which seemed to him so completely to spoil the volley that he determined to report the matter in the morning and have it enquired into. All military undertakings of whatever sort should be carried out in a smart and orderly way, an execution no less than drill; indeed more so. The sound of the volley would be heard all over the town, and by whatever the Germans did the population would judge them: in addition to this an execution was exemplary, and whatever was held up as an example either in peace or war should be perfect in every respect. A volley like that did not teach with the clearness that was desirable. It was like a schoolmaster with a cough. So thought the colonel.

Major von Wald was disgusted with it. He felt that it was especially his execution; and to have it go off like that was as though his washing were to be drying in the public eye, and one of his pieces of apparel on the line were to be torn and badly darned. Other such thoughts occurred to other Germans, for they are an orderly nation; but to nobody did it occur that the firing-party had been fired on, or that the executioners were dead and the Bishop alive.

As fast as Hlaka could lead the Bishop he hurried through the streets. They were as quiet as though nothing had occurred. Like shadows the rest of Hlaka's party ran towards the Mountain before and behind him. The streets were brighter than the pine-wood, the dark flat tops of whose trees kept out most of the moon. The Bishop wore darker clothes than did any of Hlaka's men, and that was to the good, but he had not the panther's tread of those men, nor their intuitive knowledge of danger and how to avoid it. Each man now had two rifles to carry except Hlaka, and one who carried only a pistol besides his own rifle; for they had stripped the firing-party and the officer who commanded them of their fire-arms and ammunition.

They went halfway through the streets towards the edge of the town without any sign of danger and then they heard a step coming towards them. It was too firm and loud to be

that of one of the citizens out at night, defying death. Hlaka
stopped the Bishop and turned and led him backward a little
way to where a dark shrub by a doorway might give cover.
The steps came nearer along the pavement, down the street
from the Mountain. It was only one man. Neither the
Bishop nor Hlaka spoke. Suddenly there was a cry, and the
feet stopped. The unknown man had fallen into the hands
of one of the mountaineers. Then Hlaka ran on with the
Bishop towards the Mountain; and his men all ran too, so as
to reach the edge of the town before the Gestapo should come
to enquire about that cry. They were sure to come, for none
of The Land had the right to cry in the streets at night, and
if it should be a German that would be far more serious.
But there were only two or three hundreds yards more to do,
and just outside the town the whole of Hlaka's force would
be waiting. Before they had run a hundred yards Gregor
said to Srebnitz, who was running beside him: "We can use
our rifles now, if they try to stop us."

And both unslung their rifles, for they could clearly get
to the edge of the town before any Germans that heard their
shots could overtake them. Probably all the others did the
same, but no more steps were heard, and they did not have
to fire. They all reached the edge of the town, and had not
gone far over the open country before they saw shapes in the
moonlight, which when they moved were seen to be fifty of
Hlaka's men. Then Hlaka knelt down and put on the
Bishop's boots.

For an hour they climbed the Mountain, straight up

through the heath, the Bishop in front with two of Hlaka's men to help him, and the rest of the force between him and the city; and there was no sound of pursuit. At the end of the hour Hlaka came up to the Bishop and apologised for the fatigue that he must feel, and asked if he would now go to bed for a few hours. The Bishop smiled and agreed, thinking that Hlaka referred to the bare heath. But to his surprise he saw a mattress laid down beside him and two men arranging the sheets and blankets and a pillow, and even a bolster. For Hlaka had sent several men to the houses at the edge of the town, where they had been given these things and a large number of eggs, as well as bread and cheese and butter and a few tins of sardines. The Bishop slept in his bed for over three hours, a deep and restful sleep, for his mind was too tired to dream, and his limbs were tired too. And all Hlaka's men slept in their beds, which were tufts of heath, except a crescent of sentries watching towards the town. An hour before dawn Hlaka called the Bishop and they all went on up the Mountain.

By this time the Germans appeared to have enquired about their firing-party, or to have sent men to bury the Bishop, for guns began to fire in the town, and star-shells burst over the Mountain and dropped their small gold suns, which slowly set amongst rocks and myrtle and heath all over the slope of the Mountain. As one came dropping near to Hlaka's men he called to them to stand still, and in whatever attitudes they were they stood as though suddenly frozen. The star-shell showed them up, but the night is full

of shapes, and no German picked out theirs from the shapes
of rocks and myrtles. A little shrapnel followed, but only
sent vainly against the peak that Hlaka's men had left.

When dawn touched the roofs of the city far below them,
and shone in grey windows, the mountaineers were still
amongst the myrtle. The light grew vaster and the few windows winked with orange lights of their own, and chimneys
smoked here and there; and one of Hlaka's men turned
round and gazed towards the houses, and stood awhile
motionless. With the light of dawn on his face, Hlaka
seemed to read his thoughts, for he suddenly said to him:
"We have no families. Liberty is our mother and sister and
children."

Then the man turned and went on up the Mountain. They
came again to the caves in the high peaks, and found breakfast ready for them, prepared by the few men that Hlaka
had left behind. They all ate their food by a small but welcome fire whose embers sent up no smoke, and sometimes as
they ate Iskander sang. To the Bishop Hlaka apologized for
the rude surroundings in which he sat. But the Bishop said:
"I have a pleasant view from the windows of my house, yet
never have I had such a view as this to see while I ate my
breakfast."

And indeed it was a view that held half a kingdom, for
they were just over the ridge to the north and could see the
plain below them like a great garden, whose far wall was the
blue mountains, gleaming now as though they were the
frontier of fairyland and were all newly enchanted. And in

the garden that went from wall to wall, from the peak where
they sat away to the far blue mountains, grew all the crops
that The Land had known for ages, and one or two others,
such as tobacco, which had not come till The Land was
already old. And at a great distance a glimpse of another
frontier showed, the deep blue edge of a region over which
the Italians claimed sway in error, and which the Germans
never have understood. By that frontier Tyranny halted;
and across it a man might shout *"Heil Hitler"* as loud as he
would, and, though his voice were even heard above the
boom of the other voice, would get no answer but the world-
wide derision of what an old Greek poet called the count-
less smiles of always-laughing ocean.

XXII

AFTER breakfast Hlaka showed the Bishop into a cave that
was curtained by two blankets, where his bed was again prepared for him, for the Bishop had not yet slept enough for
sufficient rest after even a quiet day.

Then Hlaka set about his preparations for the attack that,
according to the information of the barber, was likely to
come next day; and chiefly he continued his men's rifle-
practice, making them stalk pebbles at eighty yards and
shoot at them from behind cover, for he had little more time
to train his men than the Duke of Monmouth had before the

battle of Sedgemoor. A sentry made a sign from one of the crags, and Hlaka going towards him saw a man hurrying up the road from the town. It was a furtive figure that came towards them, and yet it was not the barber. After a while Hlaka sent down one of his men to guide the stranger to him from beyond the end of the road. He turned out to be a man with a letter from Trigoloutros, which he was to deliver to Hlaka. He seemed afraid of Hlaka and his men, and yet the speed with which he had hurried up from the town seemed to show he had other fears. If a man can be meaner than a spy, he seemed to be meaner than Trigoloutros, as though he were one that served spies but was not yet fully admitted by them to their company. He took off his hat before Hlaka and gave him the letter, and remained holding his hat in both hands while Hlaka read it. The letter went:

"CHIEFTAIN,

"They suspect me because I said you would come at dawn, and you did not come at the time I said. There are men watching in my street now. I know that they watch so that I shall not escape. I shall soon be questioned by the Gestapo. Men who are watched are always questioned. I may be questioned today. Come quickly, master, with all your men and rescue me. I shall be able to tell you a great deal if you bring me safely into the Mountain, for I know all the Germans' plans. Very senior officers have spoken often with me. I wish you well, and would serve you. But if you did not rescue me, and if the Gestapo ask me questions about your Excellency, I should be compelled, God knows how greatly against my will, to tell them what I have observed in the

Mountain and what I know of your Excellency's plans. Believe me, master, I observe a great deal: I cannot help it: God gave me that kind of eye. No time for more, master. Help. Help quickly.

> "Your Excellency's devoted servant,
>> "ANDREAS TRIGOLOUTROS."

"Tell him," said Hlaka, "that I will send him a verbal message."

"He is greatly pressed for time," said the messenger.

"I will send the message at once," said Hlaka.

The eye of Trigoloutros's messenger roved round the crags as though expecting some sort of hospitality, but Hlaka dismissed him forthwith. As he went, Hlaka called to Srebnitz and showed him the barber's letter and gave him a brief order. It was not often that Hlaka when giving an order ever gave any reason for it, and showing the letter to Srebnitz was an unusual favour to him.

Srebnitz went straight down the mountainside without his rifle, the way they had come that morning, a shorter way than the way by the road which went away to his right. He went all the morning among the myrtle bushes and through the plants of heath, and showed very little till he came to the town.

There he walked openly through the streets with the brim of his hat pulled down, and avoiding as much as he could the glances of any eye, his forehead hidden from view and a stubbly chin showing. Nobody recognized him, and no German questioned him, and he came to the Street of the

Martyrs. There he noticed a man in plain clothes with that
vacant look in his face which is always worn by men who
suspect and watch; but by no possible disguise could Srebnitz have made himself appear more completely in need of
a barber than by what a few days on the Mountain had
already done for him, and so he walked into the shop of
Trigoloutros, a very likely customer. Two men were in the
shop beside the barber. Srebnitz caught his eye, and looked
away and said nothing.

Trigoloutros signed with his head towards an empty chair
beside a man who was waiting, and went on cutting the hair
of the other customer. This business he hurried somewhat
and soon assured the man that his hair was exactly the right
length now; and this customer paid him and went away.
Without looking at Srebnitz, Trigoloutros asked the next
man to come to his chair and fastened his cloth round his
shoulders. This man also wanted his hair cut, and Trigoloutros cut it as fast as he could, speaking of such things as
might have been discussed five years ago by a man uninter-
ested in any public affairs.

When he had finished he half turned his head to Srebnitz
saying, "Now you, sir." And when the other man went out
these two were, as they both desired, alone in the shop. Srebnitz sat in the barber's chair and glanced hastily at the street-
door, which Trigoloutros obligingly shut.

"A shave, please," shouted Srebnitz as Trigoloutros went
to the door.

The barber came back and put his white cloth round Srebnitz and began to shave him, while Srebnitz sat silent. It was always Trigoloutros's custom to wait for his customers to speak. Srebnitz seemed uncomfortable at first under his white apron, but he soon settled down. After a while he said, "A little bay rum on my chin, please."

The barber seemed surprised at this whim, but nodded his head and got the bay rum; he never argued, and liked to leave information to come of its own accord. He put down the razor and shaving brush and came back with the bottle of bay rum. Then Srebnitz said: "I have come with a message from Hlaka."

And he lifted the apron with his left hand and stabbed the barber to the heart.

He replaced the knife and wiped his hand on the apron, and went to the door, leaving the barber dead. The lower part of the glass in the door was frosted, but the upper part was clear, and by standing on tiptoe Srebnitz could see the street. There was nobody passing. The door was latched on the inside, and he drew back the latch and opened the door and slipped through and closed it, and the latch fell back so that it could not be opened from the outside.

Then he sauntered away down the street in the opposite direction from the one from which he had come, so as not to pass the man who had seen him enter the barber's shop, for he was not yet properly shaved. On the other side there was another watcher, but he crossed the street as he came to him and contrived to turn much of his face away.

Taking the first turning out of that street to his right he much increased his pace and, turning to his right again was on his way back to the Mountain, though long streets had yet to be traversed before he was out of the town. He slouched as he went, not with the tread of an armed man or a mountaineer, and he hung his head as though he were resident in that town and the tyranny of the last week had sunk into him.

He did not expect any of the barber's household to go into the front part of his shop during his working hours and he did not fear that the door would be forced from the street or its pane of glass broken for some while. Men would not do that for the sake of a shave. But at any moment the Gestapo might come, as the barber had feared, and they would as soon break the glass as open the door, even if the latch were unfastened. So he walked as fast as he could, without making any movement that was likely to attract curiosity, or daring a pace that might be suggestive of flight.

Walking thus he passed unnoticed, wearing an abject air, utterly devoid of interest, which seemed not to attract the interest of others. Intuitively he knew that, even had he let his eyes rest upon any object as he walked, somebody would have noticed what he was looking at, then wondered why he looked, and from that would have come to wonder who the man was. After that he might have been questioned, and he would have been very near to prison then. He had not yet wiped the blood off his knife, though the barber's apron had protected his clothes, except for the right sleeve, at which he now glanced, and there certainly were a few spots on it.

And now he came to a street that ran to the open country.

He had come into the town by that very street; but it is one thing to enter a town, and another to leave it. All the world has business in a town, and any man may have reason to enter it; but what reason could a man have for going from the town into the wild open country? There might be several reasons, but the question would be asked in an observer's mind, whereas no townsman would ever ask why a man entered the town. He must leave the street unobserved. But there were people in it, so he turned listlessly out of the street to his left, and turned again to his right into another street running towards open country. Here also there were people. He tried a third street parallel to the two others, and here there were people too, and he realised that he was not likely to find an empty street in the capital in broad daylight.

He walked very slowly and very listlessly up the street towards the Mountain, wondering if he dare walk boldly into the open fields alone. And something told him that, with the edge that these intense days put upon curiosity, he could not do it. He could not look carefully at anyone, without being looked at carefully in return, either by that person or by another, but a glance or two that he did cast did not entirely satisfy him that no member of the Gestapo was among the passers-by. A cataract of wisteria poured over a garden-wall, flowering in its full beauty; all who came near it looked at the splendid mass of bloom, or at least glanced at it, but one man looked at it with an especial enquiry, as though estimating the number of blossoms and particularly admiring their shape and noting the earliness or the lateness of their flowering: so obviously was all of this interest assumed that the cold falsity of the man's heart seemed almost to freeze the beauty of the flowers and wither the image of them in other minds. Srebnitz slouched on: he dared not turn back now, and yet he dared not walk out to the open fields.

A girl was coming towards him on the opposite side of the street: he walked straight over to her and, as they met, said in a low voice to her, "It is for The Land."

She looked at him and did not speak, and Srebnitz looked at her. In times of peace and security some explanation would have been needed, or at any rate words instead of it, but in these days fewer explanations were given. Her look at him satisfied her, and when he saw that she trusted him he indicated with a slight wave of his head that he wished her to walk the way that he was going. From the bare words it may seem an insufficient indication, but dogs make such signs every day, when one of them takes another dog hunting; and, when the need arises, men and women can do as much as dogs can do. She turned and walked with him towards the end of the street, which was now not far away: beyond lay the open country.

"I have business in the Mountain," said Srebnitz as they walked together. "If I go alone the Gestapo will come after me and shoot me."

"Why?" asked the girl.

"Because they will think I am one of those who have killed some of Hitler's men," he said.

"And have you?" asked the girl.

"Yes," said Srebnitz.

"Then I will come with you," she said.

Srebnitz changed his slouching air for the air of a man who took a girl out to the fields beyond the town on a spring morning. And now there was no longer anyone in the street in front of them. Who were behind, and whether or not they followed, Srebnitz did not know, for he never looked round. He drew himself up and strutted slowly and twirled an end of his moustache as he went: looked at in front, the end of his moustache was not long enough to be twirled, but this was what the attitude of his elbow suggested seen from behind. Windows watched them, but Srebnitz had no fear of windows, only of men that lurked in the street. Unquestioned they reached the end of it, and came to the green fields in which anemones twinkled, an idyllic pair. But Srebnitz gazed at the Mountain rather than at the girl's blue eyes, as though he saw Liberty pacing the grey crags; and the girl saw that look and was content. For, though she knew that that gaze of Srebnitz would scarcely turn to her, yet she also had a vision of Liberty in the Mountain, who would one day return to the city which she had known for so long.

' They walked slowly, and no one followed. And there was no sound of any alarm in the town. Perhaps they had discovered the dead barber, and perhaps decided that he was only a barber and that the matter could wait: it was not as when Srebnitz had killed a sentry. Even though the barber was one of their spies, he was now only a broken implement, scarcely even a weapon; and unhappily Europe had many more, even though they were rare in The Land.

Talk between Srebnitz and the girl was not embarrassing, as it might have been to people acting such close acquaintance who did not even know each other's names. But both had a love of The Land that had grown so ardently now that The Land needed it so much, that they seemed almost of one family. She told him her name was Marya, and told a little of life in the town under the Germans; but mostly she spoke of the future, asking Srebnitz when The Land would be free. Srebnitz gave her some of the hope that he drew from its mighty source in the heart of Hlaka, who with his gaze fixed on the future saw so clearly The Land free, that his faith became to his men as sure as a page of history. What can fifty or a hundred men do against five thousand, with five million more if needed? thought the Germans. What can all Germany do against our sure knowledge of victory some day? thought Hlaka and all his men.

XXIII

As SREBNITZ and Marya came to the slope of the Mountain an untidiness left the fields and a carelessness took its place; or the carelessness of men gave place to the carelessness of the Mountain. One was a niggardly uselessness, with rusty tins and dirty bits of paper and many ravelled foot-tracks, the other was the carelessness of a jovial giant, losing rocks

from the crags and leaving them scattered, among them more
delicate tracks of the things that are wilder than man, and
the roads by which streams marched to find the sea. Not
only was untidiness gone, but orderliness also: nothing was
square any longer; no lines were straight, and the heave of
the slopes was of a grander design than the designs that are
planned in cities.

They came to a myrtle bush, like something strayed from
the wild to peer curiously at the work of men; and then they
came to a great many more bushes, and Srebnitz noticed
all at once that there was cover enough for him to go on
alone: he had but to stoop and go forward a few paces, and
he was a mountaineer again, invisible to any that might hunt
him, and able to remain so; thus he could pass in a moment
now from the comradeship of those who trod pavements to
the society of those that were free from all that oppresses
cities.

He paused to thank and say farewell to Marya. And as
she gazed at the dark of the myrtle, shadowed now by the
Mountain that had already hidden the sun, she heard a sound
from the strings of an instrument that they play in those
lands, and a song rose to accompany it, which was one of the
songs that the ages had drifted against that mountain, up
from whose slopes it rose on many an evening from many a
goatherd and many a shepherd-boy, a song that sounded
too light to have come down so many ages. And yet, if it
had been made of weightier things, the breath of men singing in idle hours might not with such ease have supported

it, and it might have sunk among grave arguments and old
policies, and never have come so far. Nor, if it had, would
Marya have listened to it as she was listening now. For a
moment Srebnitz listened too, then said: "It is only Iskander."

Still Marya listened, standing still.

"He is one of our men," explained Srebnitz.

But to Marya it was as though the Mountain spoke. So
perhaps it was to Srebnitz, coming home again after the
regular streets and the regulated ways of the city, which he
had now abjured. Yet, if he thought of Iskander's song as
the voice of the Mountain, he only thought, "Why should
the Mountain not speak like this?" There was nothing
magical about Iskander; certainly nothing new in the song,
which was sung today by hundreds of others, and had been
sung for thousands of years.

But to Marya this voice of the Mountain coming down the
ages was magical. A man might sing a song that was made
last week, but the song of the Mountain might be two thousands years old and yet seem fresh and new among those
ancient rocks: in another two thousand years no doubt the
Mountain would have another thought, and another song
would ring along its valleys at evening. The mood of a
mountain would not change oftener than that.

But what had all this to do with Iskander? No more than
the evening had, nor the pale moon, nor the myrtle on the
slopes of the mountain. And yet Marya in some way con-
fused all these things with him, as she saw him coming

through the myrtles now down the slope to meet Srebnitz. Some similar mistake Iskander made as he saw the girl's blue eyes gaze at him, vaguely classing her with all that was beautiful in the evening upon the Mountain, as though she were somehow kin to eternal things.

Iskander had come down the Mountain to meet Srebnitz because of his own anxiety for Srebnitz's safety, and because of Hlaka's anxiety as to what had become of the barber, for he feared that at any moment the man would betray him.

"And the barber?" were Iskander's first words.

Srebnitz pointed to his own face, only partly shaved. "He will shave no more," said Srebnitz.

"Then I must light a fire to let Hlaka know," said Iskander.

Then he looked towards Marya again. And Srebnitz told Iskander how she had helped him.

"The Germans will come to look at the fire," said Iskander to her, "and we must give you time to get well away from it."

"I can move faster down the slope than you can move up," said Marya.

"We shall be hidden before we have gone five yards," said Iskander.

And then he walked with Marya a little way down the slope. And when they had gone a little way they parted, and Iskander returned to the spot at which he had prepared some twigs for the fire. But before they parted, Marya had said some few words about his song. And Iskander had said: "I will sing it for you again if you will listen, when I get back to cover."

And she had said she would listen. Iskander sent Srebnitz on up the slope, and then lit his pile of brush-wood and ran up the slope through the myrtles, and soon saw Srebnitz again. And a column of smoke went up, and Hlaka watching from a crag knew that it was the funeral pyre of the barber. If an eagle regrets the death of a grouse or a lamb that his talons have seized, Hlaka regretted the barber. But not otherwise. As Fate has made all eagles prey upon small beasts and birds, so the tide and the trend of history, which are surely but moods of Fate, had made this man Hlaka prey upon Germans and traitors; and every day the method of his strokes was becoming more natural to him, till the stroke of the talon had barely been made by the ages more natural to the eagle. There wern so fuw traitors in all The Land that the death of the barber would be an appreciable loss to them, and it won a smile from Hlaka.

Iskander moved as fast as he could up the slope away from the fire, and urged Srebnitz, who was a little more tired than Iskander, to travel as fast as he did. Srebnitz was running, in spite of the slope, through the myrtle, when he noticed that Iskander was lagging behind. Then Iskander stopped altogether, and sitting down where a myrtle grew between him and the city, sang the song of the Mountain again, while his fingers played on the strings of his rustic instrument. The song was of a breeze that had risen up from the sea and gone inland and come to the Mountain, and that was lost in one of its valleys, and was repeatedly asking its way of an echo that it met with among the rocks. And the echo's words made no particular sense, nor did the whole story. And yet he sang it, and yet Marya listened, and it had been sung for a thousand years.

Srebnitz waited, hidden, and he waited with some impatience, for he expected the Germans at any moment to come out to look at the fire, and the two men were not yet very far from it, and still Iskander sang on. How differently time passed for those two men, every moment full of danger for Srebnitz, that most annoying kind of danger that is incurred for no cause, while for Iskander time did not seem to be passing at all. Whether music can thus enchant time, so that it can stop for a while some tributary stream of it while the main current flows on, one does not know enough about time or music to say.

XXIV

Iskander did not dally long, singing his song in the myrtles; and, before any Germans came out to look at the fire, the two young soldiers of Hlaka were far up the Mountain. The Germans that first saw it reported upon it by telephone, and waited to receive orders, then went to examine it, and returned and reported again; but they did not see Srebnitz or Iskander, and Marya got safely back to the sad town. In twilight they returned to the height where Hlaka was, with all his plans made for the next day, on which he believed that the Germans would attack as the spy had said. For spies speak the truth at times, as rich men pay out copper coins, not valuing them much, but using them as required; even so a spy uses truth. First Srebnitz went to Hlaka to report that the spy was dead. "He died while shaving me," said Srebnitz.

"That is well," said Hlaka. "He would have betrayed us."

Then he showed Srebnitz a rock on the steep slope facing the town, behind which Srebnitz was to wait next day for the Germans, a rock that would shelter him against artillery; and if aeroplanes came he was to hang a blanket from the top of the rock and conceal himself under that; and he told him to prepare the blanket the next morning as the other men would do: this was by daubing it with dampened handfuls of crumbled rock, in patches. Hlaka did not command men without knowing something of the ways of men, and he knew that the spy would have information accessible to him, and that he was speaking the truth at the time that he passed it on to Hlaka.

As Srebnitz listened to Hlaka he saw the dark shape of the Bishop coming down the grey rocks towards them. So calm he seemed, so remote from the violence of war, and that grim branch of it that is named guerrilla, that Srebnitz felt a qualm as a new thought troubled him. For the first time came the thought, had he murdered the barber? He glanced at the Bishop, then turned to Hlaka. "Perhaps I have done wrong," he said.

"When?" asked Hlaka.

"When I killed Trigoloutros," said Srebnitz.

"On this mountain," said Hlaka, "and throughout The Land till our king returns, you will obey me. Our old laws are broken by the Germans. Broken like the tablets of Moses. I make the new laws. Obey them."

Srebnitz was silent before the wrath of Hlaka, who would not have his orders questioned even though they had been obeyed; he was silenced too by the serenity of the Bishop coming towards him where he stood with a blood-stained sleeve. But Hlaka called out to the Bishop, while he pointed an arm at Srebnitz, "Is he right to obey my orders, your Beatitude?"

"Till The Land is free again," said the Bishop.

Then he saw Srebnitz standing still, saying nothing, as though yet a little puzzled. He may even have seen Srebnitz's eyes glance at his freshly stained right sleeve. And he said to Hlaka: "If you give any order without clear conscience, and he obeys you, the sin is yours."

"I gave the order with a clear conscience," said Hlaka.

Whatever weight lay for those few moments on Srebnitz's mind fell off from it now before the face of the Bishop. Srebnitz saw that he would not hesitate to condemn even Hlaka, and even though Hlaka had just saved his life, if he decided that Hlaka had sinned; but he felt now that Hlaka's authority was sanctified, and had no more qualms about his own obedience. The Bishop had walked that short way down the slope to say good-bye to Hlaka and to thank him, for he was about to ride all night to the north on a mule, with an escort of three men. At first the Bishop had refused to take any men for an escort, but Hlaka had explained that his army was actually strengthened by the weeding out of those who had not yet been trained to hit a fair-sized pebble with moderate certainty at seventy yards and to keep hidden while doing so. The three men to ride with the Bishop were the least advanced in their training, leaving a force that he could more easily handle.

There was a monastery on a mountain peak that Hlaka's men could see from where they were, sufficiently to be able to distinguish it from sky, though they could not see the monastery even as a speck on the pale blue of the peak. Thither the Bishop was to go, to live amongst the monks of the monastery, disguised as one of them, till Europe should have other laws again than the whim of Hitler. All night he would have to ride, then hide in a house all day and ride all the next night, and that should bring him to the monastery, and to calm that would be greater than any he had known since he became bishop. Not that his work as a bishop much ruffled the calm that he clung to in spite of the stress of daily work, and succeeded in holding, and then held next day against whatever cares might come, and the day after; but in the monastery all about him would be devoted to calm: there would be no need to hold out any longer; all would be peace.

But he had come to thank Hlaka, and to say farewell to him. He had not thought to have to thank any man for saving him from execution, and no phrases were lying ready in his mind for such an event, though his gratitude was sincere. Tennyson wrote:

"Not wholly in the busy world nor quite
Beyond it blooms the garden that I love."

As it were through such a garden lay the equable way of the life of the Bishop hitherto. Then in a day the garden was overrun, and a few days later he went from it to the moonlit pine-wood and the execution-wall; what to many was the real world was to him a wild strange scene which he was very glad to have viewed, though he did not associate it with reality; rather it was like some panorama, such as used to be shown at exhibitions, which he had come from his own real world to peep at for a little while. To him the master of this strange show was Hlaka, and he came to thank him.

"Thank you," the Bishop began, "thank you."

But Hlaka saw the difficulty he felt in putting his gratitude into words, and interrupted the Bishop by saying: "It is time to start down the Mountain, so as to have the whole night for riding."

The Bishop nodded his head, and Hlaka led him up over the crest and a little way down the other side, to where the three men of the escort were waiting. And there they shook hands and parted, and in the end neither of them said any-thing. All the mountaineers, unbidden by Hlaka, went down the slope to take their own farewell of the Bishop; and some way down it he blessed them among the myrtle, just as stars began to appear. Then all except the three that were to go on the long ride with the Bishop returned to the peaks, where Hlaka sat in his cave, alone, meditating his plans, and the Bishop and his escort went on in the dark down the Moun-tain, and found the four mules that were waiting; and the four men that held them came up the slope to join Hlaka.

To Hlaka, meditating his plans, it was clear that water and time were against him, and that he could not stay long in the Mountain; numbers meant little to him, nor have they meant a great deal all through history; about fighting with rifles he felt confident, nor did he bother much about artil-lery, for he believed that his men could shelter among the rocks, if they had to be out in the storm at all, and when the hottest fighting began there was likely to be no artillery, because the German infantry would be too close.

During the early bombardment that he expected, his men would be in the caves. But everything was not as easy as that, and Hlaka was troubled with the thought of Stukas. If a hundred or two hundred of these came over, it seemed to him that they would be able to pin his men to their caves until the German infantry were so close that his men could not get to their places among the rocks without suffering severe casualties; and waste of life he could ill afford, when he could scarcely even afford waste of bullets.

Had it only been the days of his father, thought Hlaka, he could have held the Mountain for ever, unseen and almost invulnerable, a home of free men, a very garden of Liberty. But aeroplanes spoiled all that dream. However attractive it was to dream of the past, Hlaka was too much of a soldier to waste more moments regretting that it was not forty years ago: and he never made vague plans to suit conditions that might be, but only adapted his plans to the actual shape of the ground that he saw before him. The most unexpected things found their places in Hlaka's plans, trifles that could not be foreseen; yet any plans that neglected them would have been vague, and Hlaka's thoughts never neglected one of such material details.

He looked now to a difficult fight, in which aeroplanes in great numbers might enable the German infantry to come up the Mountain unopposed until they were closer than he wished, as close, in fact, as their own bombs would permit.

None of these troubles perplexed Hlaka's men; they were only concerned with what was to be, which they looked on as something coming direct from Fate; only to Hlaka did the future seem something within reach, something that he might have a share in controlling. Or were all things, present and future, including the plans of Hlaka, solely moved by the land of Fate?

Sometimes Hlaka made such reflections as this, as sometimes in the night he gazed up at the concourse of stars; but further than such reflections, if there be a way further, he did not go, and even made his plans for defending the Mountain while actually pondering some such fancy, as he made his plans while gazing at the stars, without even trying to guess whether what lay beyond them, beyond the Milky Way, was infinite emptiness or infinite stars.

XXV

NOT only did the mountaineers have their supper that night by a fire, but Hlaka lit many fires, mostly along the heathy ridge to the west. A few were shelled for a while, but not the one that glowed near the caves where Hlaka's men were.

When supper was ended and the men sat still by the embers, while Iskander played his instrument and sang, the sentry at the earphones called to Hlaka that an aeroplane was coming, and presently they all heard the throb of it coming their way. But the damp blanket was not yet thrown over the remains of the fire, when the bright red burst of a shell was seen among the stars, and then there was a red row of them up there, searching for the aeroplane, and some ruby stars began to climb towards it, slowly, as it seemed to the watchers. What then was the aeroplane at which the Germans fired? For no one in The Land had artillery. It was moving northwest, this lonely pursued stranger. They heard it, and could see the pursuing shells breaking in upon the calm of the stars. Who was he that went over them in

the night? And at the same moment it seemed to occur to
them all—an Englishman.

They cheered as the throb of his engines died away to the
north and the bright shells burst no more. Their cheer was
soon lost in the night and could never have reached him: he
too disappeared in the night. But he cheered them with
thoughts of England, the old land of King Ethelred, whose
policy still survived, right down to 1939; and yet the land is
a rock on which tyranny always breaks.

Preparedness is a matter of months, but the quality that
breaks tyranny is a quality that it takes the ages to harden.
After all, no country except Germany is ever prepared for
war to the last button. The French army in 1870 was ready,
as reported to their emperor, to the last gaiter-button, but
the fuses for shells that should have burst between three
thousand and four thousand yards were not ready. Europe,
outside Germany, is indeed an empire of King Ethelred;
but something other than readiness seems to be required to
win wars: mere readiness has been tried twice in this century
and has failed.

But it was not of her armaments they thought when they
thought of England, but rather they had some sort of picture
in their minds of an island with white cliffs, against which
great seas broke vainly, for they pictured very stormy
weather round England; and within the island, flourishing
together, all the theories and policies that ever grew in
Europe, like flowers and docks in a garden that nobody
weeded, until one weed grew too strong. And of these dim

pictures all were probably different, for none of them had seen England, but the thoughts of all of them turned that way, northwest where the airman had flown, whenever they hoped for liberty; as Mahometans turn to Mecca when they pray. Not that England was quite to them what Mecca is to Islam, an original source of the faith, for they did not forget that they were older than England; and their hearts boasted, though not their courteous lips, that they had served Liberty before England had shaken off the Romans.

When silence returned to the Mountain and calm to the stars, the wine of that land and of islands near it was passed from hand to hand among those that sat round the fire, and a hum of talk arose, full of speculations and hopes about the battle that they expected the following day. Then Iskander touched his strings and the talk lulled and died away altogether, as the mountaineers felt that Iskander's gourd-like instrument said something that lay too deep for them to say, and they turned from their weak guesses about the future to those tunes of Iskander's, that had once drawn strength from the mountains which had enabled them to fly down so many ages. Hlaka retired early to his cave to sleep, and the rest of the mountaineers soon followed his example, all but the sentry.

Dawn woke the mountaineers; Aurora called them again; but she herself was saluted by the roar of a hundred guns. They fired all together from the south of the Mountain, outside the town, and a few fired from the north, two batteries that had come over the plain in the night. All the grey peaks responded, with gravity in their tremendous voices, as though they had all of them spoken of old with the gods, and slept for a long while and now spoke again, from peak to peak, and repeated the words of their tremendous lore, and muttered them over and over to themselves and once more went to sleep. At once they woke again, and this time remained long awake, vociferous and all angry, ancient voices awakened by man, as a sleeping giant may be wakened by a gnat.

Hlaka rightly decided that the Germans were a great and terrible power, and desired to show it; and he sent out only two men to watch, and kept the rest in the caves. Silence was now gone from the Mountain, utterly outcast from the calm peaks and the sky, and, as the bombardment raged on, the mountaineers began to feel a yearning for silence, as though it were a positive thing, some cloak that the Mountain wore and which sheltered themselves, till something seemed to have gone out of their lives, driven far away by guns and shells and echoes.

For an hour there was no silence in any second. Then the guns ceased all together, and a little while after that no more shells burst on the Mountain, the air screamed no more, and the grey peaks mumbled together, as though they talked over all they had seen that morning: at last they too ceased to speak, and back to the high bare slopes, as from far away, came silence. And in the silence Hlaka's man at the earphones reported a great number of planes.

This was the attack that Hlaka feared. He looked out over

the Mountain before the planes were in sight, and saw the German infantry all round him, but far away, not even visible through glasses, as a line surrounding the Mountain. But glasses showed by a movement here and there, or a flash of light from something unwisely allowed to shine, that there was actually a line of men on both sides of the Mountain; and Hlaka estimated the position and even the numbers of the line that he could not see, for he was a hunter at heart and knew that nothing in nature was in the least like what it would appear if stuffed and in a glass case, and had learned to know what a brown patch or a grey patch signified.

Then the aeroplanes came in sight, and the infantry began to advance up the slope. Hlaka had only planned to hold out till nightfall and had ample cover for his men among that great abundance of rocks against almost any number of infantry, but no rock gave perfect cover against a bomb from the air, nor was there any lore in Hlaka's blood, that the mountains could have taught his race through the ages, that could tell him how to fight against this new thing.

There must have been more than fifty planes now in sight, and Hlaka watched them uneasily, and yet with a trust which was natural to him that no difficulty would arise that he would not be able to deal with when it came: perhaps Hitler has the same feeling rising from some great store of confidence within himself, which may some day be all used up; but with Hlaka it arose from the cause for which he fought, or, if it came to him from his own confidence, that confidence was continually replenished by the cause, which was to Hlaka like an inexhaustible spring from the deep heart of the Mountain. And now bombs fell on the eastern end of the Mountain, and again the peaks spoke out with indignant voices.

Hlaka's men were still in the caves, but the German infantry were still advancing, and soon he would have to bring out his little force, to whom losses would mean so much, and he knew not how to protect them.

Had it not been for one thing Hlaka would have believed that he and all his men were lost, but he could not believe it possible that Liberty should be driven out of The Land. His belief, and more than a belief, his practical policy, was the same as the theory that Srebnitz's old father had had, that after three thousand years of liberty it could not be lost to The Land. Logically no argument could justify such a belief, but intuitions, looking deeper than logic, dimly but rightly saw some qualities in the race that had been bred in those plains and mountains, and some aid that the mountains gave them, that could no more be broken by tyranny than a diamond scratched by a sword.

And still the planes came nearer. He guessed that there were about a hundred now. Suddenly in the clear blue sky, like a white rose unfolding, a shell burst near to the planes. Another began to unfold, then more and more, and there came the sound of guns firing and, after a while, the sound of the shells. And then the crags spoke, again with deep troubled voices, and the aeroplanes that had been sailing towards him like great flocks of geese began to dart about like the flies that dance above water.

Then Hlaka saw that into his plan of battle had come something of which he had not even dreamed. The bombs that had just fallen were not like the first ones, methodically bombing the ridge: they were jettisoned bombs; the Stukas were being attacked. The white puffs in the sky were shells fired at the attackers by German batteries outside the town, and had had no effect. As the Stukas came over Hlaka they were looking for his men no longer, but were fighting for their own lives. The long growl of cannon-fire broke out as other planes dived at them, and swept past and flew on, as a bird will fly on that has missed a butterfly. And still the white puffs pursued, adding a sound to the fire of machine-gun and cannon, as though all the sky were of wood and a great fist knocked on it. Then to the roar of these noises a new sound came, a long and wailing scream, growing louder and louder, as a German plane dived headlong, and struck the Mountain, and the slope reverberated with a metallic blow.

Probably as many as sixty-four of the planes were German, and there were less than fifty English, but still the Germans were being pursued as they swept over the Mountain westwards. A long burst of machine-gun fire sounded straight overhead, and another plane came screaming out of the sky. Then the flash of a shell shone brightly beside another, and it also came down headlong. A round white object shone above it like a light in the sky and descended

slowly, a parachute in the sunlight. Cannon, machine-guns
and shells moved away to the west, and grey crags muttered
and resumed their silence and all was still again all over the
Mountain. Hlaka jerked his head towards where the parachute had come down on the northern slope, and two men
went down with their rifles.

The German infantry had stopped their advance when the
air-battle began. The two men were Iskander and Srebnitz,
and they hurried to get to the airman before he should reach
the infantry. While he got to his feet and freed himself
from his parachute Iskander and Srebnitz ran over a hundred yards, and were still out of shot of the infantry. When
he did get clear of his parachute he came up the slope, instead of going the way they expected, and very soon they
were certain of meeting him before any accurate fire could
be brought on them from below.

"Hlaka does not want prisoners," said Iskander, and
knelt down to get a steady shot.

But the airman shouted to him "English, *Anglais*," and
a few other names by which he supposed Englishmen to be
known in Europe; and some of them were accurate, but for
the accent; and one of them was near enough to what Iskander and Srebnitz themselves called his people. And Iskander
ceased to aim, but still kept him covered.

"Look here," said the airman, "you don't understand.
Ne comprenez pas. I am British. *Anglais.* You see?"

And something in his attitude towards them persuaded
Iskander and Srebnitz that he was what he said, though they

did not understand a word of English or French, and they gradually abandoned the idea that he was a German, which they had because they had not yet imagined any other people coming to the Mountain besides their own and the Germans.

"Churchill," said Iskander by way of greeting.

Srebnitz repeated it after him, and the Englishman said, "*Bonjour*, my boyos."

And so they were introduced. Still not a move came from the Germans below, on either side of the Mountain. Their orders had been to wait for the peaks to be bombed, and they were waiting for the return of their air-force. The Englishman continued to talk to the mountaineers. When he spoke English they sometimes understood him, because he understood what he was saying himself, and that somehow conveyed to them a part of his meaning; but sometimes he spoke French, perhaps because he did not understand it, and felt that people who did not understand English must understand what an Englishman did not understand; but indefinite thoughts are hard to analyse and he may merely have felt that whereas no English words were like any that these people spoke, the French, being nearer to them, might have some words that were the same, and he might chance on one of them while he spoke.

"Your name, old boy," he said after a while, pointing his finger at Srebnitz. "*Nom, nombre, nomen;* N or M, you know." And one of these words reached Srebnitz's understanding and he told his name, and the Englishman did to his name what his countrymen have done to pneumonia and to Lake Tsana, finding too many letters in them and discarding one, and ever afterwards called him Rebnitz. Then he pointed similarly at Iskander saying *"Et votre nom,* my fine fellow?" And he got the name of Iskander, which had already been passed on from man to man through many centuries, losing a syllable here and a letter there on the way, and had once been Alexander. Then he stopped and pointed vigorously at himself, saying *"Moi, je suis Malone."* And they understood him.

"Strictly speaking," he said, "I'm neutral. *Irlandais,* you know. But those blighters down at the guns didn't seem to understand that."

"Churchill," said the two men.

Then Hlaka came down the slope towards them smiling; for he knew that his men would not dare to bring him a prisoner, and that therefore the stranger was British. And the Briton saluted and said, *"Bonjour,* Chief." For no deep insight was needed to see that Hlaka was master here.

"I am Hlaka," he said.

"Lanker, eh?" said the Briton, doing what most Englishmen have done to Hlangwani. *"Moi, je suis Malone."*

XXVI

A LITTLE later Malone sat in a cave, deep in conversation with Hlaka. Two interpreters had been found, the cook and

Gregor. And between them they explained Hlaka and Malone to each other.

"You can't stay here, you know," said Malone. "Not if the Germans keep on at you. What you want to do is to get away to the north. There's plenty of room for you in the mountains over there."

What Malone felt was that the British Empire was the leader of the free nations, and that, as he was the only Briton present, he must obviously do the best he could to represent the empire in a humble way, and therefore to lead. So he explained to Hlaka what he ought to do, and the grim old chieftain listened.

"The Germans won't attack yet awhile," said Malone. "They'll come up later in the afternoon."

"How do you know that?" asked Hlaka, when it was interpreted to him.

"I had a good deal to do with horses," said Malone, "before I joined my present outfit, and vicious ones among 'em. And, you see, I always had to know beforehand what a vicious horse was going to do, or he'd get me down. So I suppose I developed the knack. Anyway, I usually know what the Germans are going to do."

Hlaka pondered on this, and it took some pondering, even in the original. It was a very mysterious statement by the time the cook and Gregor had done with it; and the mystery attracted Hlaka. And there was a certain downrightness in Malone, such as had won the Battle of Britain. And there were not only the qualities that our airmen showed in that fight, nor the humble home-guard down below, and the A.R.P. wardens and fire-guards, but a certain doggedness that was shown in battle by the charwomen of London, and many another body that had no regimental badge, and whose work cannot possibly be argued to have won a battle. And yet the battle was won, and could not have been won without them. What quality these possessed and how it won the battle is beyond the power of definition; but, whatever it is, Hlaka recognized it in Malone, and seemed to see in it a lure for the winged Victory, whom the London charwomen had already lured from the sky.

"You'll be all right when you get to those mountains to the north," Malone went on. "You'll find some of our men there. Some of them got cut off, and they're there yet. And there's a lot of your own people up there too with them. You'll be all right when you get there, right as rain. *Très bon comme la pluie.*"

"It's a hundred miles to those mountains," said Hlaka.

"That's the trouble," said Malone. "*Quelle domage*, I mean. And there's Germans all the way, dotted over the plains like fleas in a dog's hair. Did you ever have a dog, Chief, that was bad with fleas? I tell you it's the devil. Well, the Germans are like that. You'd better go by night."

"It's a hundred miles," said Hlaka again.

"Yes, I know," said Malone. "What you want is a lift. A Sunderland flying-boat could take fifty of your men and get you there in about half an hour. I must call up one of

them for you. But the trouble is the damned thing can't
land. There's a river running out of those mountains that
would be just big enough for it, but there's no water that I
know of at this end."

"There's the sea," said Hlaka.

"You couldn't get to it," said Malone. "Fleas too thick in
that direction. No, you'll have to keep north. There's a lake
in that direction, a lake that would do nicely, but it's forty
miles away. Can you do forty miles in a night?"

Forty miles in a night was a remark easily made by a man
who was used to flying four hundred in an hour, but it was
scarcely a remark to make to infantry.

"Yes," said Hlaka.

The cook and Gregor wondered. But Malone knew men
better than he knew foreign languages and saw that Hlaka
meant what he said, and so bothered no more about it.

"Very well," said Malone. "If you can get to the lake in
the night a Sunderland will come for you just before dawn,
if I can whistle it up. That's better than flying all the way
in the dark. Have you got a sending-set? A wireless that
can send out messages?"

"No," said Hlaka.

"Well, plenty of your people have," said Malone. "We
must get in touch with them. But you want to watch those
Germans, you know. They'll be doing a bit of mountaineer-
ing soon."

He knew that Hlaka was well prepared, but felt that, in

his capacity of sole representative on this mountain of the
empire that was organizing most things, he ought to remind
Hlaka of anything that needed to be borne in mind.

"I have sixty-two men waiting for them," said Hlaka,
"and rifles for four more when they come."

"Then perhaps you could give me one of the rifles," said
Malone, "and I'll do a bit of shooting when the time comes."

Much of this conversation was helped out by signs, and
Malone now went through the motions of aiming with a
rifle, and pointing to himself and said, *"Pour moi."*

Hlaka called, and a rifle was brought, which he gave to
Malone, who looked it all over and said: "I can have a fine
time with this."

Hlaka explained his theory of only firing at under a hundred yards, so as to preserve ammunition. But Malone said
lightly: "Oh, we can send you plenty of that."

It was a long while since anyone else had brushed aside
Hlaka's words, but Malone's casual remark lighted new
hopes in Hlaka. If the English could replenish his ammunition like that he could go on fighting until Hitler was tired.

"Well, what you want is a Sunderland," said Malone.
"Can you get in touch with any of your boys who could send
a message for me by wireless?"

"I can send messages all over The Land," said Hlaka,
"but even I do not know where the wireless transmitters are.
Of course it is death to be found with one."

"Then can you send a message that will be passed on to
one of them?" asked Malone.

"Yes, I can do that," said Hlaka.

"What code do you use?" Malone asked him.

"I have a code that I use in the town," said Hlaka, "but there's no one with a transmitter there, because the Germans would locate it at once. And nobody to the north has the key-word. So I shall have to send a messenger."

"Too slow," said Malone. "You should keep pigeons. But never mind. I can send a message in plain, if you can get it passed on to him. I've no key-word either."

"I can send it by helio," said Hlaka, "and it will be spread over the country till it reaches the man with the sending-set."

All this conversation took some time; especially as the two interpreters did not always agree. Complicated technical terms about wireless were the easiest, because in many cases the English word for it was used in that Near Eastern land. Then Malone wrote out his message, addressed to the number of an aerodrome in Egypt, which simply said: "Look for fifty men fishing for carp. If you're waking call them, mother dear. Dick."

Hlaka looked gravely at it when Malone gave it to him, and then handed it on to Gregor and the cook. It did not seem very plain to any of them, but it might be to the Germans, and this had to be considered with every message.

"Will the Germans understand it?" he asked.

"Yes," said Malone, "in a hundred years. They'll work it out and get the right answer; but we'll be gone by then. The second part of it is taken from a poem known to almost every Englishman, and is about early tomorrow morning. That of course will mean dawn to them. The Germans know well enough what books Englishmen read and which poems are popular with us, but all their things are docketed and put away in drawers, and it will take them a little while to find them, before they begin to work it out. The other part is simple enough, or will be to the Sunderland people: they are always thinking about water, because they can't come down anywhere else; and fishing rather implies water. They know where I am, because some of them will have seen me shot down, and there are only two bits of water anywhere near here, and carp suggests fresh water; so it must be that lake. They'll work that out all right, and so will the Germans in a hundred years."

So Hlaka helioed the message over the plain to the north, repeating it again and again. And the Germans carefully took it down and translated it and worked it out, and got at the meaning sooner than Malone had said, but not that day nor that night. And the message, like all Hlaka's messages, went over The Land, and came that afternoon to the men who had a hidden transmitting set, and a minute or two after that it was arriving in Egypt, and the C.O. of the crew of a Sunderland knew that Dick Malone was alive in the Mountain and that he wanted fifty men to be picked up and taken somewhere.

"What are you going to do about tanks?" asked Malone.

But a report had just come to Hlaka that the Germans were moving again, and this aroused the old chieftain, so that some of the awe fell from him which he had felt for his liaison with England that had been brought to him by Malone, and now he pointed to Srebnitz's air-gun leaning against a wall of the cave, and said: "I will shoot them with that."

And Malone, seeing that his question had been a little too childish, and that the old chieftain would be questioned by him no more, replied: "And just the thing for them."

XXVII

THE Germans were now coming up the Mountain on both sides, and had already climbed up at the western end, where none of Hlaka's men were, and were moving along the ridge. At the same time a tank came up the road, from the end of which it would be able to sweep the rocks of the crags with an enfilading fire at men facing southwards. In under two minutes each of Hlaka's men had gone to the rock from which he was going to fight.

More shells came up from the town and from the plain to the north, but ceased even before any Germans came within the distance at which Hlaka allowed his men to fire. Malone was firing away long before the Germans came within the range that Hlaka allowed to the rest, with the disregard for ammunition such as came natural to a man accus-

tomed to firing with eight machine-guns, and with some
success too. But Hlaka did not check this representative of
England, for he had been much impressed by Malone's easy
assurance that plenty more ammunition would be sent him.

The Germans were closing in towards the same point, evidently knowing accurately where Hlaka's men were. Then
the air over the Mountain shook with a blow that even the
Mountain itself seemed to feel, and air and Mountain
seemed to shudder a second time, and then, more lightly, a
third, and then a fourth; and far peaks shuddered too, and
roared with their great voices. It was the German tank, and
the culvert, and several yards of the road, going up in an explosion of guncotton. The broken culvert and the wreck of
the tank, lying across the wreck of the road, would prevent
any more tanks coming up the Mountain that day. The man
who exploded the mine never got back to the rest: Germans
were close in front of him, and on two sides, by the time he
fired it: he shot five of them, and was bayoneted.

And then the line of Germans on the northern slope came
close to the mountaineers, and just outside the ordinary
range of hand-grenades Hlaka's men began to fire. The Germans could not see them, and could not rush their positions,
because the slope was much too steep. And they were too
much out of breath after their climb, to make accurate shooting even when they had anything to fire at, while Hlaka's
men were lying still. About the same time, or very soon
after, the men coming up from the slope on the other side
came under fire.

Hlaka's men were completely surrounded by about eighty times their numbers, but the odds were all in their favour. The Germans were too close for the artillery to give them any more help, and their aeroplanes seemed to have been hunted away. Among the first five shots that each of Hlaka's sixty men fired there were very few misses, not counting the shots of Malone, who was more prodigal with bullets. Such losses as that could not go on for long without destroying much of the German line. Nowhere was the slope in that part of the Mountain easy enough for them to do that last eighty or ninety yards while the defenders reloaded their magazines, and they soon lay down behind rocks, as the mountaineers were doing, and began to fire more steadily than they had done hitherto, but still with very rarely a visible mark to fire at.

As they heard the long roll of their own fire, duplicated by mountain-echoes, they felt they were doing some good, but they were unable to cross the steep and rocky space between them and their opponents. This firing went on for a long time, while Hlaka's men continued to fire only when they saw a German, or some part of him, who had not been able to conceal himself. Sometimes during a lull in the mountaineer's firing, or when it had ceased altogether, owing to there being no more visible targets among the Germans, a few Germans would crawl forward; and these were invariably killed.

When Malone, who was above the rest of them, could see nothing more to fire at within three hundred yards on the northern slope, he crawled a few yards through the rocks and looked down on the other side, and did some shooting in that direction.

At last the German fire lulled, not because they had not plenty of ammunition, which Hlaka greatly envied them, but because they had been ordered to cease fire; and Hlaka saw that whoever commanded them had a new plan, the first one having broken down. Hlaka was glad that they had ceased fire, and for a very curious reason. But the reason was simple enough: the Germans were his sole source of ammunition, and he did not like to see them wasting it.

As the day wore on and the Germans neither advanced nor retired, Hlaka soon saw what the new plan was: the steep slope that the Germans could not climb with unseen marksmen opposing them would not be at all the same obstacle at night, when both sides would be invisible; they would lose many more men when they left their shelters, even by night; but what was left of them would, with such numbers in darkness, be able to overcome the mountaineers, even if they used no more than their bare hands. There would be a moon, but that would not show the sights of a rifle; even late twilight gave insufficient light for accurate shooting. And the day was wearing away. Already splendid colours shone low in the western sky. The Germans were lying perfectly still, and waiting.

Hlaka knew they would move soon after nightfall, but did not expect them to attack at once; he expected them rather to move their entire force first, up to where their

front line lay about a hundred yards from his own men, so
that the attack when it came would be in the great mass that
the Germans love. His own plan was to break through
their line after dark and before it was strengthened, on the
northern slope below the precipice, where they would least
expect him. There would not be much time to spare, unless
he relied on the Germans not to attack till late in the night,
and that would be to lean too heavily upon Fortune.

So, as the brief twilight faded, he began gradually to
withdraw several of his men to the edge of the small precipice, which they did by crawling in the dim light among the
rocks, more and more as the light grew dimmer. Among
these was Srebnitz. There was no firing now and Srebnitz
saw a German officer standing up and looking towards them
with his field-glasses. Every question that arises in the kind
of war in which Hlaka's men were engaged has to be answered; and, as no man can know everything, guesses are
of value, and an actual part of such warfare. Srebnitz
guessed that in bad light a man can still see through field-
glasses, and he guessed rightly.

He was about to crawl to Hlaka to tell him that the
movement towards the precipice was being observed by this
German, when something struck him about the man's figure.
He was well over the distance at which Hlaka allowed men
to fire, even in good light. Srebnitz took another look at
him, but in that light could make out nothing for certain.
He crawled to Hlaka, who was only a little way off, and told
him they were being observed. But there was something

more than that, and he asked Hlaka if he might look through the field-glasses which the chieftain always carried. Hlaka handed the glasses to him and Srebnitz put up his head and looked, and the late evening seemed to brighten a little bit, and he saw clearly the German officer's heavy figure, and at that moment the German's glasses went down and he saw the red face and cruel eyes of von Wald. He turned suddenly to Hlaka.

"May I shoot?" he said.

Hlaka shook his head.

"But it is Major von Wald," said Srebnitz.

Hlaka reflected a moment. He had two machine-guns, but he looked on them as a careful man looks on spendthrifts, and he had not used them yet: in a few minutes they would have fired away all the ammunition he had. But von Wald's name was in the book; it was a case for the machine-gun. So Hlaka sent a message along his line of men to the man who had charge of it, and he crawled up with the machine-gun, and Major von Wald was still there.

Hlaka gave Srebnitz permission also to fire his rifle, although the distance was quite a hundred and fifty yards, but not to fire it until the machine-gun had begun to fire. And he himself came with the two men to the rocks from which they took aim. Then von Wald sat down behind a rock and was out of sight, while all three men watched the rock with their weapons ready. Time seemed to pass slowly in the still evening, and still the light faded.

Once more von Wald stood up and raised his field-glasses.

Srebnitz could only just see anything of the foresight when he had the whole of it in view. Knowing that the sight he took would make the bullet go far too high, he aimed below the major's knees. Suddenly the machine-gun began roaring in his right ear and he fired, and unheard by him Hlaka fired too. The major went down. Srebnitz could not be sure whether he was hit or not, till he heard Hlaka say to one of his men: "Scratch his name out of the book."

XXVIII

A PLANET shone, and soon the stars came out. Hlaka, interpreting the few sounds he heard, coming up the slope through the hush, knew that the Germans were closing in all round from below, but there was no movement yet from their firing-line.

As soon as it was possible to move his men unseen at a hundred yards he moved them towards the edge of the small precipice, walking now, though stooping, and taking as much care to go unheard as lately they had taken to go unseen. No moonlight showed as yet on the northern slope, and the precipice showed black. There Hlaka waited a few minutes, then had the ropes quietly let down and sent his men down them, two or three on a rope at a time, while several hands above took the strain off the roots of the trees to which the ropes were fastened.

Srebnitz was among the first of those to go down, with his rifle slung from his shoulder and various provisions strapped about him. The dark and the emptiness seemed cold to him. Then the rope nearly burned his leg; and sooner than he expected he touched the ground among myrtles. The noise that he made, and that his comrades made, seemed to him to be certain to be heard by the Germans, if they were only eighty yards away, but no shot came from them.

At the foot of the precipice he waited anxiously, with a few others, to protect the men on the ropes if the Germans should move. But still no sound came from the Germans, and more and more mountaineers came down the ropes and Srebnitz soon felt the confidence that is given by numbers. This was the thinnest part of the German line, for the precipice was unclimbable, and most of the Germans had moved away from it either to left or right, and most of those that did approach it had been easily seen from the high edge and shot, but Hlaka expected to meet with supports and reserves as he went down their slope.

He drew up his men in two ranks, shoulder to shoulder, and led them straight down through the myrtles. They met only two Germans: a few shots were fired, and they were through the line; and that was two more rifles for Hlaka's men. Half a dozen shots did not entirely give away Hlaka's plan, but he hurried for fear that the Germans should find it out. Two hundred yards further down he met more Germans, men coming up the Mountain to strengthen the line that had surrounded him, and he went straight through them with a burst of firing on both sides. He lost one man here, killed or wounded; there was no time to see which. Indeed, like Napoleon in Egypt, and, as they say, some German field-marshals, wounded men on either side were details that did not fit into Hlaka's plan; his own wounded were a sacrifice that the sacred cause for which he fought might well demand, as he saw it, and the German wounded were something he never spoke about, and about which his men never troubled him.

The second burst of firing must have shown clearly the way that Hlaka was taking, but he moved his men over the ground with the speed of mountaineers, which he hoped would outdistance the Germans, quite unfamiliar with his native mountains. Not all his men were mountaineers, and several had joined him only the day before; but Hlaka's pace was the pace of the fastest, and he left the slowest to make themselves his rearguard, and to follow as they could. Very lights were fired, turning the night to a queer green, full of flickering shadows, but they did not discover Hlaka's men. And they came to good oak-scrub and felt they were safe. The line closing in on the peaks was now wholly behind them, and no Germans were likely to be ahead of them any longer, except the men with the batteries in the plain. But Hlaka knew exactly where these were.

They went on unmolested and the slope became gentler, and the dark bulk of the Mountain rose behind them, and before them were all the stars. While Very lights still soared and flickered vainly behind they came to the last sweep of the slopes that draped the Mountain. Then Srebnitz heard a voice saying in words with no meaning to him, for they were in a foreign language: "Well done, Chief. You've come to a road."

And sure enough their feet touched a road, which is always a strange and welcome thing to men who have been for a time in the wilds. It was not long since Srebnitz had seen a road, and yet even he felt the thrill of it. Travel for a time in the wilds, and you will perhaps meet no more thrilling thing as you come away. What a wonderful thing a desert would be in a city. How children would play in its sand, how young men fare out into it from the last street. Think of the camels waiting where the buses end their journeys. The noise and the smoke behind, the quiet and the mirage before. As strange as that is a road to the men of the wilds.

Even there Hlaka did not wait for his rearguard, but dropped connecting files to keep in touch with them, and got his men into fours and marched them down the road at a pace of five miles an hour.

"How are you going to do the forty miles tonight, Chief?" asked Malone.

Hlaka beckoned up Gregor, who interpreted, and Hlaka told Malone his plan, a plan that had been in his mind ever since the time when he had briefly said that men could do what wild sheep had done. Men had not the strength nor the speed of the wild sheep, but man's brains made up for that. Whether he has used his brains wisely, who can say? But his brains have certainly achieved wonderful things, and a motor's engine is one of them. From one of the farms that supplied Hlaka's needs, as all the farms in The Land were willing to do when they could, Hlaka had obtained a lorry, which was not far away on the road along which they marched. It was a small lorry and could not hold more than twelve men with their rifles and few provisions; but Hlaka's plan which he now told to Malone, with the help of Gregor, was that the lorry should pick up the last twelve men, and take them twenty miles and then return for the last twelve again, and take them twenty miles also, again returning.

Hlaka had calculated that during the night there would be time for the lorry to take all his men on one journey, they would rest in the lorry and continue to march when set down. He calculated that his men could easily march twenty miles in the night, in addition to which each man would do twenty miles by lorry.

"A simple sum, Chief," said Malone as soon as he understood Gregor's interpretation. "Forty miles."

Malone approved the simple arrangement and felt that, as the only Briton present, he should express that approval. "Very good, Chief," he said.

And very soon the lorry passed them, going without lights, to pick up Hlaka's rearguard.

All that night Hlaka's men marched or sat in the lorry; marching, after the first half-hour, at an easier pace. Hlaka did not expect to meet any Germans, as they were all concentrated on the Mountain; and he was not molested during his night-march. Once the lorry met a cycling patrol, consisting of a German corporal and two men, and they were all shot by the men in the lorry. One of the bicycles was damaged; the other two were taken by Hlaka's infantry. Sometimes the men that marched rested briefly beside the road; but none of them rested long, except in the lorry, and before dawn they saw the pale cold gleam of the lake to which Hlaka had said he would come, forty miles away from the Mountain. There they waited, while time dragged slowly. But, however slowly time passed over the waiting men, dawn seemed to be coming swiftly, and there was no sign of the Sunderland.

Hlaka looked towards Malone, and Malone was uneasy, but he smiled confidently; and Hlaka saw his uneasiness under the smile and said nothing.

Hlaka cast his eyes about the countryside now emerging from night, trying to find some place where his men might hide and rest during the day. For a lorry could not go down the road by day unobserved by the Germans, and his men would have had to have fought one of those battles that he avoided, a battle in the open such as history notices; nor could they have marched another twenty miles at all without rest. More and more of the country came out of the darkness, while Hlaka observed its crops, its rocks and its bushes, planning where he would put his men if the Sunderland did not come.

Hlaka sent the lorry into a grove of trees that was not far

from the road. Day was coming up rapidly. The men looked at each other; there was light on their faces, and the night that had covered them was all gone. A flash came over a low hill to the right, that was from a cloud immediately over the sun, and Hlaka decided to take his men from the lake to hide them as well as he could.

At that moment there came a hum like the sound of the pulse in one's ears. Hlaka listened, and all his men. The sound grew. All of them turned their eyes to the south, from which the sound was humming, and there came the Sunderland. In barely a minute it had come down to the lake and its floats plunged into the water, and Malone was smiling a perfectly genuine smile. Hlaka looked at him, and Malone knew without an interpreter what Hlaka wished to say.

"She doesn't ride very deep," said Malone. "We can all walk out to her."

It was a chilly morning on that grey lake; but there was no other way.

XXIX

"Tell him where you want to go, Chief," said Malone. For the pilot was standing at an open door above a little flight of steps.

And Hlaka spoke to Gregor, who called out to the pilot

telling him of the Blue Mountains and the river. The pilot nodded, and Hlaka's men began to walk through the reeds, and walked on through open water holding their rifles over their heads, while the crew of the Sunderland refuelled it from the great number of petrol-tins that were piled up where passengers usually sit.

"Have any trouble coming here?" shouted Malone to the pilot.

"No," said the pilot. "We've a few fighters watching over their aerodrome. But we'd better get off quick. Fifty men, please. All standing."

"Hope my message explained itself," said Malone.

"Not very well," said the pilot. "Why didn't you go on with the quotation and say something about the brightest day in all the glad what-do-you-call-it? That would have clearly indicated tomorrow."

"Well," said Malone, "I thought of it, but that might have meant the first of May, and as the first of May is so damned close I didn't like to risk it."

"I see," said the pilot. "Perhaps you were right. Well, get them in as fast as you can."

And the dripping men climbed in. Hlaka had lost altogether five men in the fight and, when the Sunderland was full, only six were left by the road. The two that had bicycles Hlaka told to hide by day and come on at night, all the way to the Blue Mountains, and the other four were to come by night as far as they could in the lorry, and to leave it and come through the country as they could, if they felt unable to get the lorry through. Then the door was shut and the propellers started just as the sun came over the hills to their right, and a golden curtain of spray waved past the windows, a curtain that seemed to be caught in a raging tempest, which suddenly dropped away and they floated in air.

Earth looked beautiful, just awaking from sleep and casting off gauze wraps, as the mist appeared, thickened here and there by early fires from chimneys of cottages and from little encampments, which a breeze drew gently away. Dark mauve lay the shadows of clouds on the green of the land that the fifty men had fought for, and in a few minutes they saw all its mountains. Then the soaring plane went into the skirts of the clouds, and nothing was to be seen for a while from the windows except these light-grey shapes.

Thence they came out into unshadowed sunshine, into a world such as they had never seen before, a world of white plains with white peaks rising amongst them, and steel white islands drifting in bright blue. They had not looked long at this serene white world, when again a mist closed round them, and the shapes of clouds went wildly raging past, and earth appeared again, and the mountains quite close. A river gleamed ahead of them, the earth slanted, and soon two waves of spray were rushing past the windows.

Malone was delighted; he had moved an army without a casualty; there was plenty of cover along the banks of the river for fifty men to hide till nightfall; and the Blue Mountains were only five miles away. But no smile lit the brooding face of Hlaka.

"You're all right now, Chief," said Malone. "Plenty of

cover here, and even a house over there, and the mountains barely five miles away."

Gregor translated, but Hlaka made no reply.

"There's plenty of your own people there, Chief," said Malone. "More than you think, and some of our people too. And all well armed."

But this good news brought no gleam of a smile to Hlaka.

And then he spoke: "My daughter and two sisters are in that house," he said. "And the Germans are looking for them."

"It would be hard living for women in the Blue Mountains," said Malone thoughtfully.

"Yes," said Hlaka.

And then a thought came to Malone. "We can't wait here long, you know," he said. "But that house is little more than a mile away. We could wait half an hour. If you could get them here, we could do something better for them than that." And he pointed to the Blue Mountains.

Hlaka thought for a moment. "Egypt?" he said.

"Yes," said Malone. "And worth seeing. But we could find a better climate for them than that. The *khamseen* can be a bit of a curse, you know. These Sunderlands run to Natal and, any time there was room, we might take them. We've every kind of climate in our bit of an empire, and they'd do grand in Natal."

Hlaka thought. Natal. A land where there were no Germans. Then he nodded his head.

"Well, send some young fellow to get them, Chief," said Malone. "And make him run."

Hlaka nodded again, and beckoned to Srebnitz and pointed out the house to him. "I sent my daughter and sisters there," he said. "Bring them here quickly. Give me your rifle."

Srebnitz paused to say something; he did not know what, for a great flight of thoughts was rising up in his mind.

"Quickly," said Hlaka.

So Srebnitz turned and ran, and reached the house in ten minutes. To see Sophia again! He was out of breath, and a little bit out of his mind, or at any rate his mind was too much dominated by thoughts of Sophia to be able to function in the way that uninspired, unstimulated, dull minds function. His mind was irradiated by visions of her, and immediately darkened by fears that she might not have reached the house, or might have left it, or even might be dead, and then irradiated again by memories of her smiles. Amongst these hurrying moods Srebnitz knocked at the door of the farmhouse, and it was opened by Sophia herself. And her two aunts sat inside, calm as ever. Others were there, whom Srebnitz scarcely saw. But beyond Sophia's face and around it he saw a large room, rather dim, full of many things that helped to hold back the light, but which somehow seemed to strengthen the feeling of home, that hung all over the room, as though chairs and tables and curtains and one or two barrels, and many odds and ends of a southern farm, were those little lesser gods that the Romans knew by the name of lares and penates, gathered about the altar of the great fireplace. Amongst all these Srebnitz saw in a single flash the elderly farmer who was evidently master of the house, and his wife and three or four cats and two dogs.

"Sophia," he said.

She smiled at Srebnitz, then turned to introduce him to the master of the house.

"My uncle," said Sophia.

But there was no time.

"The Chieftain says you must come to the river at once," he said. "There's an aeroplane there."

Isabella and Angelica looked up.

"He says the Germans know you are his sisters," continued Srebnitz. "He wants you to come at once."

Isabella never even spoke. She went straight out of the room to gather up her belongings, and one glance at Angelica as she went brought her too.

"The plane cannot wait long," Srebnitz called to them.

"Then I'll get ready too," said Sophia, and ran out of the room.

There had been no argument or discussion where Hlaka's words were concerned.

"Come in," said the farmer.

But Srebnitz stood at the door, not daring to waste even a few moments on receiving hospitality.

"You fight with Hlaka?" asked the farmer.

"Yes," said Srebnitz.

"He married my sister," said the farmer.

"Yes," said his wife, "she came from here."

So that accounted for Sophia having come to this house.

"We are going into the mountains," said Srebnitz.

"You'll find plenty more up there," said the farmer, "all well armed. The Germans will never get you out of it. And you'll get all the provisions you want. We all of us send them up to the men in the mountains."

"Are there any Germans between us and the mountains?" asked Srebnitz.

"Sometimes there are a few," said the farmer. "But they are very cautious, and, if you meet them and start a fight, the men in the mountains will come down to help you."

"We must go quickly," said Srebnitz, for those were his orders from Illaka.

But at this moment Sophia returned, and her two aunts followed her. They had brought few enough possessions to this house, and they soon gathered them up. Farewells took up some time, and Srebnitz drew back from the door so as to make no leave-taking, which would have added many more seconds to the delay, and the farmer came too, carrying bundles for Sophia's aunts.

Srebnitz ran with Sophia, in order to encourage Isabella and Angelica to go their utmost pace. But, when they were moving as fast as they could, he dropped behind with Sophia, knowing that it would be no use to the waiting plane if he got there five minutes before they did. Confident that he and Sophia could overtake the aunts when they chose, he dropped back with her.

And that short walk, with no time to spare for loitering, was the idyllic time of their lives, the time to which they would long look back, with the scene that was now about

them undimmed by the years; the rocky land, the green
maize growing in fields, and, shining upon the wilder land,
the anemones. Words said by Srebnitz too, and Sophia's answers, echoed on in his memory, to linger there probably
when old age shall have come to him, and when he has
learned a graver way of talking, outlasting there the pro-
nouncements of statesmen, the inventions of savants, the say-
ings of wise men, and even the words of songs. And no less
clearly these words in Sophia's memory rang on with undy-
ing echoes, echoes that always heartened her in the long days
of waiting for The Land to be free. And one could record
here these memorable words, but that they were too trivial,
and would never gather about them in cold print the magic
with which they were all enchanted, a magic that seemed to
Srebnitz to come from the hills and anemones, and butterflies and the light of the sky, and scores of other ingredients
out of which Love brews his charms. But the general pur-
port of their talk was that they would remember each other
for ever, and that they would be married as soon as The
Land should be free.

XXX

FAREWELLS were brief at the river-bank. If a wandering
Stuka came by there would be no concealing the Sunder-

land, and it had not the speed to escape. So every minute brought risk.

"Well, Chief," Malone called out from the plane, "let us know anything you want. We'll send you a wireless transmitting set, and all you'll have to do is to ask."

Before his words could be translated he was back inside the plane, to allow Isabella and Angelica to come in, whom two men had carried from the river. Srebnitz carried Sophia. And that was a memory that Srebnitz treasured for two years in the Blue Mountains.

The moment the three ladies were on board the engines started, and Hlaka's men waved their hats and gave a cheer for the victory that they knew in their hearts they would win, to hearten the ladies as they left their native land; not that they heard it above the roar of the engines, but they saw by the faces of the men that they were cheering and that they saw victory shining through the mist of the years to be.

Then the curtain of foaming water hid everything for a while, and when it fell away Isabella, Angelica and Sophia saw come true a dream with which they were all familiar, for the poets of their country had dreamed it for three thousand years, and taught the dream to others, until the scientists dreamed it, and then the workers; and at last man flew. They saw their loved Land below them with all its colours and shapes, and every detail except altitude, so that they could not always distinguish between bushes and trees, or between mounds and mountains.

Soon, like sheep-dogs about a lonely sheep, to fit one

metaphor to their purpose, or like gnats in summer above a horse's head, if a metaphor is chosen to fit the eye, there appeared an escort of Spitfires to see the Sunderland past the German aerodrome near the city, and safely out to sea. So small and high they were that the three ladies never noticed them; and Malone, who stood beside them, did not point them out, seeing no reason to inform them of details of the protection of the British Empire, letting it suffice that that protection was over them like a shield. A few more minutes and there came into sight the deep-blue Mediterranean. Soon The Land lay behind them and the three ladies who saw the dreams of old poets come true now saw, just as Shelley had seen it, either with his two eyes from some high cliff or from some airy height to which his genius had soared:

"The blue Mediterranean, where he lay,
Lulled by the coil of his crystalline streams."

For strange streams slept along the floor of the sea, wrapped round by purple seaweeds, which, from the height at which they were, showed as clearly among the greens and the blues as they could have been seen by a diver. What they were none of the ladies knew, nor could Malone tell them. Perhaps they were inland rivers far out to sea, and cutting their beds through the floor of it and heaping those beds with seaweed, as silks and satins are brought to adorn men's houses. Or they may have been tracks of old storms that have long since rested, leaving the weeds where they had led them on their wild adventure.

Sophia was satisfied with the sheer beauty of the sea, but Isabella wanted to hear something of the cause of these purple streams that ran amongst cobalt green, and turned to enquire of Malone; but Malone had gone away to wring out his wet shirt.

They went through the morning over the inland sea, and at noon saw the square white shapes of the houses of Alexandria, and crossed the Nile's greatest luxuriance, till the pyramids came in view; things older than The Land, older than its whole story. There was something breathtaking in that, something inspiring awe, as does a great precipice. Sophia and her aunts saw no especial beauty in them, but they were like precipices among the ages, looking sheer on abysses of time.

A few miles from these stupendous monuments they alighted on the water. There in Cairo they were cared for with many of their compatriots, whose men repaid the debt by fighting in the desert. In those days all the jacaranda was blooming, beautifying Cairo with its great masses of mauve-tinted blue. They went right up to the pyramids, to see their mystery closer. And there they stood, the memorials of one of those great struggles that a man makes every now and then, out of bravado, ambition or any other whim, against the things that threaten him; Cheops against oblivion, Hitler against liberty; both of them winning at first, both of them holding out still. And then they went to the

Sphinx and tried to make out what she seemed to be saying to the dawn. So old she is that the dawn has grown weary of her at last and has moved a little away from the spot at which on midsummer's day she used to smile in front of the face of the Sphinx. And when the bloom of the jacaranda fell, and the scarlet began to flash upon the flamboyants, places were found for them on one of the Sunderlands that was to fly to Natal. Malone came with an interpreter to say good-bye to them.

"Tell them," he said to the interpreter, "that they'll be right as rain in Natal. No Boches there to bother them, and we'll bring them back as soon as we've driven the heilhitlers out of The Land. And tell them that the Chieftain will be all right. There are lots of men with him, and we'll keep them well supplied. And men like him and them will be about the only people that will be able to manage those mountains; the Germans won't have a chance. And, well, that is about all."

And next day Sophia and her aunts started south in another Sunderland. Again they followed the Nile, and, stranger than a strip of carpet from a house-door across a London pavement, stranger than one strip of carpet going the whole way through a great city, went the green strip of cultivation beside the Nile, sheer through the desert for hundreds and hundreds of miles; till they lost sight of the Nile and crossed wild desert, where mountains were, with streams in all their valleys, widening as they went downwards, and meeting tributaries on their way, golden streams only of sand, such as Death might drink at a banquet given at noon in that land to the powers that hated man.

They came to the Nile again, and saw upon the Nile's right bank the four great images guarding the door into the hill that was hollowed to make a temple, when dawn was a little south of where it is now. Green palms appeared and they came to Wady Halfa, and rested there that night, and went on at dawn over that tremendous desert, and crossed the Nile on the way and found it again at Khartoum, flying low enough, where the Blue and the White Nile meet, to see the colours of the two rivers.

Two hundred miles more of desert, and life began to appear, scanty and sere at first, as though awed by the nearness of Death in his vast realm of Sahara. They passed by Abyssinia on their left, undisturbed by any enemy, for the Italian empire in Africa was at that time crumbling away. They came to Malakal, and there a deadlier enemy than Italy lurked, the Yellow Fever, but it did not harm them. Next day they came to Uganda. There was no memory of any desert there, and grasses in the marshes of the Nile grew tall enough to hide elephants.

And then the herds of animals appeared, that still roam Africa, though every year the frontier of their wild lands recedes further; warthogs with tails straight up galloped through grasses, and herds of elephants stood with their great ears stretched to listen, and their tusks shining; and crocodiles lay motionless on the mud of the river with their upper jaws lifted up, while hundreds of hippopotamuses

made life one endless bath. None of these animals had ever
been seen before by any of the three ladies, and one of the
officers of the Sunderland, who knew something of their language, wondered what they would make of so strange a
scene.

"You wouldn't stand much chance down there," he said
to Isabella, pointing down to the elephants, and to a pair of
rhinoceroses that had just come out from the reeds where
the crocodiles lay.

"I expect I could manage," said Isabella. "I have lived
amongst Prussians."

They saw the Nile foam over the Murchison Falls. They
saw their shadow trailing across Africa, sometimes upon the
earth and sometimes on clouds, surrounded by a rainbow;
but it always came with them. They came down on the
Great Lake among blue water-lilies, and crossed it and
rested at Kisumu among frangipani trees, and went next
day over Kenya at fifteen thousand feet, where mountains
give to the air some of their rugged quality, so that their way
lay over invisible obstacles. They saw at a long distance
the great head of Kilimanjaro, which appeared a black head
streaked with grey, for the mass of snow that crowns him
was somehow lost in the sky. They came down out of the cold,
suddenly into great heat, and were at Mombasa. Thence
they crossed Zanzibar and came to Dar-es-Salaam, and
walked in its tree-lined streets and went on again, and
flew low across the Rufigi river; and in the river lay like a
dead monster the German cruiser, the *Koenigsberg*. The

officer that knew the language of Sophia and her aunts said nothing, and none of the others even pointed; they merely flew the Sunderland low, and the three ladies, exiled from their Land by the vast might of Germany, could see the great ship with shell-holes in her side, lying there lost in Africa.

At Lindi they came down again among blue water-lilies, and rose and crossed the Ruvuma, and so left the British Empire and came to Mozambique. Next day they crossed the country of Mozambique and were in the Empire again, sailing over Zululand. For the last thousand miles and more they had moved over forest, with small round clearings in it, and in the clearings groups of little thatched huts.

And so they came to Durban, a city of splendid trees, planted in orderly rows along its streets, and wild patches of African forest still preserved, which were there long before the oldest house in the city; and behind it to the west its suburbs rising, garden by garden, over all the hills.

And here they waited, and are waiting yet, for the storm to abate which has driven Liberty so far from what to them is her natural home. And their waiting is cheered, and their exile mitigated, by the hospitality of Natal. And yet they live for only one thing; and no grandeur of scenery or beauty of flowers that Natal has to show can ever draw them away from the news at the hour at which they are accustomed to listen. And as great birds in this very Africa wait, motionless in their patience, for the death of some large beast of prey, so Isabella and Angelica wait for the end of

Hitler; and of late they see many signs that that is near, and with these signs they comfort Sophia.

Meanwhile Srebnitz with Hlaka in the Blue Mountains, and men of an army far better equipped than the one that he first joined, lives in a great cave, of which there is a tradition passed down from man to man, like traditions we have of old houses in England, saying that Queen Elizabeth slept there; but this is an older Land, and tells not of a queen but a god, and says that therein lived Pan. And there Iskander sings to Marya a hundred miles away, since love can use new inventions as well as dream old dreams. For Malone has kept his promise and sent a transmitting-set to Hlaka, and a message has been sent to Marya to tell her when to listen.

Against these mountains the Germans can make no headway. Sometimes they send Bulgarians and Italians to try their hands, but they do no better; the mountains are too steep, and Hlaka's marksmen grow better as the months go by, until he has let them fire at over two hundred yards. And remnants of English and New Zealand regiments that are still up there sum up the situation, when they say of the Germans: "They haven't a dog's chance." And some of them try to translate that into French, believing it to be nearer to Hlaka's language than their own.

There they wait with the past behind them, safe with all its glories in the great cave of Pan, and before them the future, lit by the wings of victory flashing in each man's dreams, or, in visions that hope often brings them, spreading like golden meteors across the sky of The Land.